THE DAUNTLESS

STAR LEGEND BOOK FIVE

J.J. GREEN

INFINITEBOOK

So faithful in love, and so dauntless in war…

— Lochinvar, Walter Scott

PART I

1

———

Taylan hated herself for what she was about to do but she had no choice.

She checked herself over for a final time. She'd discarded the fortune-teller's garb she'd been wearing for weeks with relief. She'd hated dressing up like a fairground display. Now the Britannic Alliance had retaken its homeland, she was back to plainer clothes as well as boots and a warm coat—essential requirements at this time of year in West BI. She'd also cut her hair.

Her clothes were second hand and worn. She hadn't wanted to spend her remaining funds on anything fancier. She hoped she didn't look too shabby for the receptionist to take her seriously.

A stiff wind blew in from the sea as she walked along the harbor front, undoing her previous efforts at combing her hair. The sea was unusually rough. Waves crashed into the walls and spilled onto the promenade. She dodged the tongues of water that reached across her path.

As she arrived at the West BI Parliament, her heart was

beating fast, though not due to exertion. She had to succeed today. Her children's lives could depend on it.

The building's gigantic roof extended over the broad walkway, slowly undulating, mimicking the movement of the ocean it faced. Wide steps rose up to the glass-fronted entrance. She had known about this place all her life but she'd never been here before. She'd never imagined she would have a reason to visit it.

Taking a deep breath, she mounted the steps.

At their top stood four security checkpoints. She picked one and walked through the archway. No alarms sounded. She emerged into the lobby.

Parliament was busy, unsurprisingly. The Britannic Isles had been in turmoil since Kala Orr had been forced to give up control of the country. The BI government had returned to its seat in London and begun issuing laws and regulations like they were going out of fashion, while at the same time repealing nearly everything Orr had put in place. But compliance among the Crusaders was patchy at best. There were regular protest marches and disturbances. Fighting and looting had become commonplace. From the conversations she'd overheard, most of Orr's followers were deeply skeptical of what they were being told. They didn't believe their Dwyr had married Arthur and handed the reins of power to the former government. They suspected she was being coerced.

In the time Taylan had lived in Crusader society, her estimation of them had sunk low. Their beliefs were bizarre and they were gullible to a ridiculous level. But she had to give them credit when it came to their understanding of the current situation. They were absolutely right.

Navigating the crowd, she approached the reception desk. The shortest line was five people deep. She waited impatiently for her turn.

When it came, the receptionist looked her up and down before saying, "Yes?"

The woman greeted every other visitor before Taylan with a *Good morning sir/madam. How can I help you?*

Self-consciously, Taylan smoothed her hair. "I'd like to speak to Mr Jonte."

The receptionist's lip curled. "I'm afraid that won't be possible. What did you want to speak to him about? The government has several help pages on its website. I can point you to the right one."

"I don't need the government's help. This is a personal matter between Mr Jonte and me."

"If you know him personally, then I'm sure you can discuss your business with him on your own time." The receptionist leaned over to address the person behind Taylan. "Next, please."

She stepped to one side to block the woman's view. "I can't speak to him outside his office hours," she blurted. "I've tried."

She really had. She done all she could to find out where Jonte was living and how to contact him. But now he was a member of the new government, he was well-protected from ordinary people like her. Anonymous limousines with darkly tinted windows left the building each evening, whisking the officials away to their homes. Vidcalls and mails were routed to secretaries who vetted them before they reached their intended destinations. No attempt she'd made to contact Hans had succeeded. She knew it for a fact because he would have replied. She was certain. She'd made it clear he was her last resort.

The receptionist replied, "Then I'd hazard a guess Mr Jonte doesn't wish to speak to you."

"He will if he knows it's me. Please, just call him and give him my name."

The woman's expression turned hard. "As I said, that won't be possible. Stand aside, madam."

"No. Call Mr Jonte. It'll only take you a few seconds. I swear to you, he'll see me once he knows who I am."

"This is ridiculous," muttered the receptionist.

Her hand moved under her desk. She was summoning security.

"All right," said Taylan. "You don't give me any choice."

She reached into an inner pocket of her jacket and pulled out a fist-sized grenade before placing it on the desk with a clunk. The receptionist's eyes nearly shot out of her head. Her chair squeaked as it scraped backward over the floor tiles.

The grenade was made of materials scanners couldn't detect, and it had cost all of Taylan's remaining funds.

A stillness and hush spread out across the lobby like an earthquake with Taylan at its epicenter. Quiet footsteps sounded around her as the people waiting shuffled away.

At last, she had the receptionist's full attention. "Call Mr Jonte. Now."

Giving a small cough, the woman reached for the headset hanging around her neck and moved it onto her ears. At the same time, her gaze flicked to somewhere beyond Taylan's right shoulder.

She lifted the grenade above her head. "If anyone comes any closer I'll detonate it." She glanced behind her. Two security guards were poised mid-step.

She turned to the receptionist. "Now."

The woman spoke quietly into the mic. Was she really speaking to Jonte? Or was she only playing for time?

The receptionist nodded and gave a tremulous smile. "Mr Jonte will speak to you."

She lifted the headset and stood up. Leaning over the desk, she handed it to Taylan.

She checked behind her again. The security guards had

managed to come closer while she'd been distracted. It didn't matter. As soon as she spoke to Jonte, he would sort out the problem. He would assure them she wasn't dangerous.

One-handed, she slid the headset over her ears and adjusted the mic. "Hans?"

The line was silent.

Feet pounded on tiles as the guards rushed up. A large man's fist enclosed her grenade-holding hand while her other arm was twisted painfully behind her, the force lifting her onto her toes. The guard holding her arm pivoted her and began marching her, dragging her, toward the exit. The other guard maintained his firm grip on her hand.

"It's okay!" Taylan protested. "There's no need to...*arghhh!*" The pressure on her arm was unbearable. If she didn't do something, the guard would break it or dislocate her shoulder.

She went deliberately limp, forcing every muscle and tendon to relax. As the tension left her body she slumped, pulling her captors down with her. The agony in her shoulder briefly increased but then the hold on her arm loosened. She wrenched her wrist free. Turning, she kicked one of the guards in the knee. He completed his passage floorward, his features twisting in pain. The other guard continued to grasp her hand wielding the grenade as if his life depended on it.

She elbowed him in the face, once, twice, three times. His nose flattened beneath her jutting bone, spurting blood. Yet he still didn't let go.

The other guard was rising, heavily favoring his uninjured leg, his face pale and sweaty.

"Let...go...of...my...," Taylan muttered between her teeth, punctuating her words with a punch to the first guard's face. He was only inches away, too close for her to get her full strength behind the punches, but by the fourth one he began to lose consciousness.

As his grip faded, she pulled her hand free.

The other guard leapt at her.

She threw the grenade into the crowd.

Shrieks and screams echoed in the chamber and the people stampeded.

She ran.

Pain lanced from her back as needle-sharp points pierced her coat and embedded in her skin. A bolt of electricity ran through her and every muscle in her body clenched. She toppled like a felled tree to the floor.

2

———

The cell door opened.

"Visitor for you," said the prison guard sourly, making it clear he didn't think she deserved visitors.

When she saw who had come to see her, she understood the guard's attitude. She felt like a bratty kid who'd got what she wanted by throwing a tantrum.

"I'm getting a sense of déjà vu," said Hans Jonte as he walked in.

"Thank God," she said, rising from her bunk. "I'm sorry about—"

"Sit down. You aren't going anywhere."

"Huh? Why? I thought you'd come to get me out"

"You're under the Britannic Isles' law now, Taylan Ellis, not medieval Crusader territory. You can't threaten the lives of hundreds of people and then walk out of prison because you know someone of influence."

She slowly lowered herself to her bunk. "Damn. What's going to happen to me?"

Tears started to fill her eyes. She blinked them away angrily. She'd come so far, done so much... "But I didn't hurt anyone."

"The two guards you assaulted might not agree with you on that," said Jonte, pulling out the cell's only chair from beneath a table and sitting down.

"But the grenade was fake," she went on. "I was only using it to get people to pay attention."

"You certainly succeeded." Jonte leaned forward and rested his elbows on his spread knees. "It's nice to see you, despite the circumstances."

She nodded, mumbling, "You too."

It *was* good to see him. In the time they'd spent together following their escape from Morgan and Dwyr Orr's slimy son, she'd come to know and like the former head of the Secret Intelligence Service, but her mind was on her problems. The knowledge that Jonte wasn't able to have her released immediately had come as a terrible shock. She'd achieved one aim only to fail her other, more important, one.

"I have to say, however," Jonte continued, "a simple vidcall or mail would have done if you wanted to speak to me. Terrifying governmental staff and visitors to the Parliament was overkill."

"I tried!" she protested angrily. "Don't you think I tried? You don't realize it, but your support staff surround you like an impregnable fortress, protecting you from ordinary people like me."

"I wouldn't call you ordinary," said Jonte with a smile. "What could be so important you needed to commit an act of terror to speak to me about it? I'm guessing you didn't only want to pay me a social call."

"No." She hung her head. "How long are they going to keep me here? Do you know? Do I have to go on trial for what I did?" The threat of a long sentence loomed. She'd already wasted precious days just trying to contact Jonte. She couldn't afford to waste any more time.

"The prosecution service hasn't decided yet. I promise I will pull every string I have to help you, but I'm not a miracle worker. Now this is the Britannic Isles once more, everyone is subject to the laws of the land. Taylan..." he reached out across the narrow cell to touch her knee "...why did you want to talk to me?"

Her tears flowed beyond her control, dripping onto her lap. "Money. I need money. I have to get to Australia, and I don't have enough money to buy a ticket."

He sat upright. "That's *it*? *That's* what all this is about?"

"That's it," she said bitterly. She'd spent all the money she'd earned as a Royal Marine getting to Ireland and buying passage to the West BI coast. The latter had been the greatest expense. Paying someone to risk their life to transport you to an invaded land was expensive.

"But when I was Mayor of Abertawe I gave you plenty of money."

"And I gave it all to the Resistance. I couldn't risk being caught with lots of cash on me when I was pretending to be a fortune-teller. It would have looked suspicious. Besides, do you remember the whole 'nearly-being-hung-by-Morgan' episode? Did you think I had my bra stuffed with Crusader notes through all of that?"

He snorted a laugh. "I didn't really think about it, I have to admit."

She drew her sleeve across her face and looked up. "You remember about my kids? I found out they're probably in a Crusader camp in Australia. Now Orr's ceding her territories to the Alliance, I don't know what'll happen to my son and daughter. I have to get over there and find them as fast as I can."

"How can there be a Crusader camp in Australia? It was never under Earth Awareness Crusade control."

"A friend of mine—Major Wright. Do you remember him? He was one of the officers with Orr and Arthur at the victory parade."

"Yes, I know who you mean. I'd already met him in Jamaica. Not the most reliable BA officer ever."

She frowned in confusion but ignored this tidbit to continue, "He uncovered a child trafficking operation while on patrol off the coast of Australia. The Crusaders were bringing children in from countries they'd conquered. As far as I know, no one's found where they were taking them or what they were doing with them. My kids have to be there. I know it. I've searched everywhere else."

"I see. Orr must have been laying the groundwork for another invasion. Have you checked the Reunite Directory?"

"Yes!" she exclaimed. "Of course I have. Do you think I'm an idiot?!"

One of the first acts of the new government, after re-installing a countrywide net, had been to create a site where separated families could post information to find their missing loved ones. She had scoured it several times daily without success. Wright's tip was her strongest lead.

"All right," said Jonte placatingly. "I was only checking."

"Do you have children?"

"No, I've never been married. I..." Sorrow flitted across his features, then it was gone. "I don't have any children."

"Then you don't know how I feel. I have to get to Australia, Hans, soon. Isn't there *anything* you can do to help me?"

"Major Wright must have informed the Australian authorities about his discovery. I'm sure they're doing all they can to locate the camp. As soon as they do, your children's names will appear on the Reunite site. I can keep an eye on it and let you know if their names appear."

"No! That isn't good enough. I have to go to Australia. Who knows how long it'll take the authorities to find them? They're only little. They might not even remember their names anymore, not if the Crusaders have forced them to use new ones."

The thought of Patrin and Kayla amongst the cultists, being indoctrinated with their weird beliefs and probably mistreated, caused sobs to well up in her chest. Her shoulders shook. Suddenly she was weeping uncontrollably. She'd been holding herself together for so long, focusing on her search, battening down her fear and despair, but she couldn't control her feelings any longer. Jonte's news that she could be convicted of terrorism and imprisoned for an unknown length of time had dealt the final blow.

She was dimly aware of him shifting from the chair to her bunk and putting an arm over her shoulders.

"I will do what I can," he murmured.

3

———

Hans mentally added the task of trying to find Taylan's children to his long list of things to do as he left the prison. The days since the re-taking of the Britannic Isles had been full of activity, and they promised to be equally full for years to come. Setting aside his concern over his friend's plight, it was a good feeling.

Worming his way back into a governmental position had been surprisingly easy. The disturbance to the functioning of the country had been significant, and few people on the ground could be trusted. It was lucky for Taylan—in a sense—that she'd committed her desperate act today. If she'd come to the West BI Parliament next week, she would have been too late. He was moving to London on Friday. He might not even have heard about her stunt except as gossip at an after-work drinks event.

He resolved to do all he could to help her. He owed her his life, though to be fair he had been in danger because she'd implicated him to Morgan. No matter. Taylan was brave, honest, resourceful, and competent. She would be a wonderful asset to the BA someday, but not until her children were found and she was out of prison.

The door to his chauffeured vehicle opened and he climbed inside.

"Parliament House, sir?" asked the driver.

"Yes, Kahlil."

Hans turned on the seat back interface as the car pulled away. As usual, the roads were mostly clear of traffic. The Crusaders had done a great job of destroying most motorized conveyances. Consequently, the price of vehicles was ridiculously high and few could afford them. It was another situation to be remedied as soon as possible, along with the repaving of roads fallen into disrepair. An efficient transportation system was essential to a strong economy.

Fixing the roads was an easy endeavor compared to many the BI government faced. The greatest challenge was dealing with the disgruntled Crusader population, which wasn't accepting the new regime at anything like the desired speed. Orr had opened the country's gates to her hordes as soon as she'd invaded, and now her people formed the majority. Though the displaced native population had begun to return or come out of hiding, they were outnumbered by their invaders. Property disputes between the returners and the people who had stolen their homes were vicious. Several murders had taken place.

A very long road lay ahead.

Yet he was sanguine. No successor to the murdered King Frederick had even been discussed yet. The BI monarchy seemed to have been forgotten in the haste to resume control of the country and strip Orr of her powers. He would be the last person to mention the lack of a king or queen.

But he was forgetting. They had King Arthur, the Dwyr's 'consort'. Arthur was the reason no one in the government was mentioning Freddie's successor, whoever that might be—probably some distant cousin. If the Isles needed a king, Arthur would fill the role.

Hans chewed his lip.

The car stopped, and he broke from his reverie. They'd arrived. His door opened.

"Thank you, Khalil."

"Will you be leaving at the usual time tonight, sir?"

"I imagine so. I'll let you know if I plan to stay any later."

Hans stepped onto the sidewalk and through the security entrance at the back of Parliament House. Now he thought about it, he realized Taylan had been right about him being difficult to approach. The rear of the building was only accessible by governmental vehicles and the entrance was heavily guarded. Both were essential requirements in the face of the social unrest. And all incoming communications to him were reviewed by staff. Her messages to him must have been screened out. If she hadn't pretended she would blow up the building, he might never have heard from her again.

He walked the quiet, carpeted passages to his office, passing only a couple of staff members on his way. The behind-the-scenes atmosphere of the building was a marked contrast to the urgent, noisy crowds packing the lobby. Every day, people called on their local government to solve the many problems of their new lives. He was grateful to the people who protected him from the masses, though Taylan's experience was an unfortunate side-effect.

He opened the door to his outer office and was greeted by his smiling secretary, Walker.

"Was your trip successful, sir?"

"Not as much as I would have liked. Anything important come in while I've been gone? Anything from London?" He'd been waiting to hear official confirmation of his re-appointment as head of SIS. He'd deliberately acted as though there was no question over his resumption of his role, but he still needed the Government's stamp on his new contract.

"No, I'm afraid not."

Hans inwardly cursed. Bloody office politics as usual. They were making him wait in order to show him his place.

"Will you be leaving this weekend regardless?" asked Walker.

"Yes, it's just a formality."

Hans moved to the door to his inner office.

"We'll be sorry to see you go."

He grunted a reply.

"Oh, sir."

"Yes?"

"You have a visitor. I showed him into your room. I hope I didn't overstep, only it didn't seem right to make him wait."

Hans turned from the door and walked to his secretary's desk to speak to him quietly. "That was a mistake. Please do not repeat it. I shouldn't need to point out to you that anyone who enters my private chambers could have access to—"

"It's a rather important visitor, sir," Walker blurted.

"It doesn't matter how important they are. You cannot risk sensitive information getting into the wrong hands." Hans sighed as he returned to his office door and silently thanked the stars he would be leaving behind the West BI Parliament and its amateurish staff soon. He was not so dense as to leave classified information easily accessible, but the principle mattered.

He went into his room.

A large figure sat on the visitor side of Hans's desk. Though he could only see the man's broad back and shaggy hair that hung below his shoulders, Hans recognized him in a heartbeat.

"Arthur! What a surprise!"

The old king rose to his feet and strode over to Hans, his large sword swinging at his side. Reaching down, he grabbed

Hans's hand in his massive paw and pumped it. Then, as if for good measure, he thumped Hans's back. "It's good to see a familiar face. I'm sorry for intruding. I hope you aren't too busy."

"I am always busy," Hans replied, hastily crossing to his desk before Arthur could find another part of his body to attack in greeting, "but never too busy to see you. Please, sit down. Did my secretary offer you something to drink?"

"Yes, thank you."

As Hans seated himself, he surreptitiously took in the king's appearance.

In the early days of their acquaintance he'd taken care to forge a friendly bond with Arthur, as he did with every important person he met. He'd tried to do the same with Kala Orr, but she'd either sneered at or entirely ignored him. Arthur had been different. He'd been polite and open and almost eager to make friends. Hans had sensed a deep melancholy in him. It was probably something to do with the severing of his close relationship with Merlin—figuratively and literally, considering he'd sliced off the alien's head.

The two historical figures were famous companions, and their relationship had continued into modern times. Then Merlin had revealed that, to him, the king and the rest of humanity were only pieces in a vast, elaborate game his species played.

The epiphany would have destroyed anyone's friendly feelings.

Arthur's depressed state seemed to have worsened since Hans had last seen him. The king's shoulders sagged and he looked disconsolate. He seemed older, too, though it was only ten days or so since he'd last seen him.

"What are you doing here?" asked Hans. "It's a long way from London. I didn't realize you had business in West BI or I would have invited you for dinner. There's still time, of course, but I'm sure you're here for another reason. A king rarely has time for frivolities. How can I help you?"

Arthur raised sad eyes to meet Hans's gaze. "I'm not sure that you can, my friend. I don't have a good reason to see you, other than the desire to have a conversation that doesn't involve reconstruction, controlling disruptive citizens, or regulating food supplies. Things were simpler in my time."

"Ha! The affairs of high office are often more tedious than the general public thinks. I'm sorry your duties are so wearing."

"In truth, I'm complaining about nothing. They've stopped talking to me about those things, probably because I couldn't give them any answers. I'm a man of action, Hans, not policy."

"Indeed you are. That's a fair assessment, I'd say, though we haven't known each other long."

"I'm feeling more and more like a puppet these days. They tell me to go to the re-opening of an old BI establishment and I go. They tell me to sit in on a meeting but say nothing, and I do it. They pull on my strings, and I hop."

"I can see how that would drain a man after a while."

"Drain is a good word to describe it. It's as though my life energy is leaving me, drip by drip." He sighed and passed a hand over his eyes.

Hans had an inkling about Arthur's visit. "Does anyone know you've come here today?"

The mischievous grin of a young child broke out over the king's face, turning it youthful once more. "I slipped away this morning. Someone had mentioned I could use my... What's the name for this? I've forgotten."

He held up his wrist, revealing a pink scar about a centimeter long and a barely discernible square bump beneath it.

"Ah, you've been given a credchip."

"That's it. Someone mentioned these could be used to

purchase passage on the rail vehicles. It was difficult to figure out how to do it but I managed in the end. I had to get away, if only for a day or so. I'll go back soon, I suppose, though I don't really want to."

He sighed again. "My heart isn't in this new role the Britannic Alliance has given me. I agreed to pretend to be the Dwyr's consort because they told me it would save lives when they retook the Isles. I think they were right and I'm glad of it. But pretending to be married to Orr was a lie. I'm not comfortable with living a lie."

"I can see that," Hans commented. His earlier work building a relationship with the king was paying off. Though he was mildly sympathetic about Arthur's plight, he was also wondering how he could use the information.

His visitor's cathartic flow appeared to have dried up. Arthur was silent. To encourage a few more drops, Hans asked, "How has Dwyr Orr behaved toward you?"

Arthur shuddered. "I believe she must truly be a descendant of Morgan as they say. It shows in every glance, every expression, every word she utters."

"A human descended from an alien? I'm not sure that's possible." Biology wasn't Hans's strong suit, but he was fairly sure he was right. Two different species couldn't reproduce, especially not if one were not even from Earth.

Arthur's expression became shamefaced. He swallowed before replying, "It is possible." He paused but didn't elaborate. "All Orr cares about is power and her son, exactly as Morgan did. She's evil, Hans. It worries me that she's supposed to be the supreme leader in the BI, even if only in name. But they seem to have her under control. When we're in public she behaves toward me as directed. Out of the public eye she pays me no attention whatsoever, for which I'm grateful. I want nothing to do with her."

"You certainly have it hard. I can see why you needed some time off, and I'm pleased you came to see me."

"You're the only person I know who isn't using me for their own ends. No, that isn't true. Major Wright is another friend of mine, and Taylan Ellis. But TJ returned to his normal duties days ago and I haven't seen Taylan since we left this city in the heli. Have you seen her? Do you know how she is?"

"I have seen her, just now," Hans replied, his heart quickening in excitement.

A plan was forming in his mind. The cogs of a complex scheme were slotting into place. All that was needed to get things moving was a small push.

4

———

Taylan curled on her side in her cell and wept. How could she have been so stupid as to think it didn't matter what she did to see Hans? Of course he was right. You didn't just walk out of prison in West BI because you knew someone important. Things hadn't worked like that before the invasion. There was no reason they should work like that now.

How long would it be before she could get to Australia? The sentence for terrorism had to be long, even for fake terrorism. It would be years before she was released. Patrin and Kayla might not survive, and if they did she might never find them.

Her eyes were nearly swollen shut and her throat was raw but she couldn't seem to stop crying. In all the days of darkness since she'd stupidly handed her kids over to another's care, she'd never been so low.

She almost didn't hear the lock of her cell door open and someone walk in.

Jonte had come back.

She sat up and pointlessly wiped her sodden face and runny nose with her hands.

His expression told her all she needed to know about how she looked, but she didn't care. She sniffed. Had he come to say he would get her a good solicitor or she might get a reduced sentence? "Tell me you have good news," she croaked.

"I have very good news," he replied, smiling.

There was something about Jonte, something secretive and scheming, that always left her feeling on edge. She could never fully trust him. Even now, when he seemed to be helping her, she guessed his efforts were for his own benefit too.

"Is it the best news?" she asked, hardly daring to dream she might not have to wait years to be released.

"It is the best news."

She leapt up. "I can leave?!"

"Not quite yet. Your case still has to be processed. But you should be allowed out by early tomorrow at the latest."

She grabbed him in a tight hug. She didn't care if he was helping himself too. It didn't matter as long as she was set free. "Thank you! Thank you so much. I'll never forget this."

He chuckled and patted her back. "It isn't me you need to thank."

"Oh?" She released him, confused. She didn't know anyone else who could have manipulated the justice system to make an exception for her.

He stepped to the open doorway and beckoned someone outside.

A familiar figure stepped in.

"Arthur!"

The dim light hit him unflatteringly, creating lines on his once-ageless face. Yet if, as Jonte implied, he was responsible for her release, he was the most wonderful sight she had ever seen. She grabbed him into a hug too and fresh tears poured from her eyes, tears of relief. "I don't know what you did or how you did it, but I'll be grateful forever." She released him and glanced at his sword before adding, "You didn't have to kill someone, did you?"

"No," he replied. "No one has died. I'm pleased to see you and glad I could help."

Hans laughed. "*I* might not have the influence to override a lawful arrest, but who would question King Arthur, newly returned to resume his throne?"

Taylan said, "I'm guessing...nobody?"

"Exactly," Jonte replied, looking like the cat that got the cream. "Not yet anyway, though I impressed upon the local police they must expedite their process. I told them the king is leaving in the morning and he wants you to accompany him."

"Huh? I can't go anywhere with Arthur. I have to go to Australia as soon as I get out of here. Or did you only tell them that to make them hurry up?"

"I do want them to push your case through the system quickly before anyone higher up in the chain notices what's happening. There is a chance someone could object. We need you out of prison and both of you to be long gone before that happens."

"I don't understand." She looked from Jonte to Arthur and back again.

"I am coming with you to Australia," said Arthur. "Hans explained it very well. I'm unhappy in my new role. You know me, Taylan. I'm not cut out for politicking."

"You're coming with me? But..."

Everything was moving very quickly. She'd gone from the depths of despair to elation and now to utter confusion. The idea of *King Arthur* accompanying her on her search for her children had never entered her wildest dreams. How would that even work? She couldn't imagine him trekking through the Australian bush, his sword clanking at his side.

Besides, he was supposed to be Dwyr Orr's consort, a new head of state leading the BI into a peaceful future.

"I don't think you can just walk away from your job, though," she said, before checking with Jonte, "Is this a condition of my release?"

"No, you will be released, barring any last-minute interference from London."

"Phew!"

"The question is," Arthur said, "what is my role now? Am I the king here or aren't I? If I'm the king of the BI, then I can do what I please. If I'm not the king, then I have no authority and shouldn't be treated as if I have. I shouldn't be signing documents or attending opening ceremonies or sitting in on meetings about subjects I don't understand."

"I can...see your reasoning," She glanced at Jonte, wondering what was going on.

Yet it was obvious, in a sense. Though she didn't understand why, it was clear that Jonte had put Arthur up to this. The king would never have come up with a plan involving him neglecting his duties on his own. Her release from prison was only a fortunate side-effect of Jonte's scheme.

"So you're going to help me find my kids?"

"I know you've been searching for a long time," said Arthur, "and Hans told me you have a good idea where they are now, only you lacked the means to travel there. I have plenty of money..." he raised his wrist to show her his credchip scar "...and you're welcome to all of it. I never cared for gold in my previous life. It's also better not to travel alone in the lawless lands beyond the BI's borders."

"The lawless lands?"

He had no knowledge of Australia. That was obvious and not surprising. In his time, no one in the West had even known of the country's existence.

"The place you believe your children were taken to," he explained.

"I know what you mean," she said. "I'm just not sure it's a good idea."

His face fell. "I see."

Jonte said, "You need to understand, this expedition would be a way for Arthur to take a break, to get away and regenerate."

"But right now?" she asked. "When things are still so unsettled? Do you really think the BA will agree to it?"

"They don't need to agree to it," Jonte argued. "He's the king. They have no authority over him."

She wanted to ask him why he was doing this. Why did it suit him to have Arthur out of the country? Didn't he want the BI to return to normality?

"I will check in with the people in London from time to time," said Arthur. "Hans said it will be easy even though Australia is very far away."

"Yes, you can use comms," she said, "but we'll be in the outback, and we don't have military-grade equipment. We could be out of touch with civilization for days at at time."

Arthur tapped his credchip. "I can buy anything we need."

She was about to voice another objection but she snapped her mouth shut. What was she doing? Jonte said she could go free whether or not she agreed to take Arthur with her, but he was devious. He might only have said that to appease the king. Arthur wouldn't like it if he thought she was being coerced, and Jonte was definitely looking uncomfortable at the direction of the conversation.

"Arthur, I would be happy to take you with me. It's a deal."

The king grinned like a five year old.

5

Catching the low-orbit shuttle to Australia meant they would be there in less than an hour. If Taylan had been relying on her own funds she would have caught the regular plane, considerably lengthening the flight time. But now she was accompanied by the actual King of the Britannic Isles, no less, money was no object.

The BI Government had been generous with his allowance. Her eyes had popped when she caught sight of the balance in his account as he paid for their tickets.

Her release from prison hadn't come through until midnight, after the last direct flight had departed, so they were catching the early morning AM shuttle. As they waited to check in, she threw worried glances over her shoulder. Surely the BI authorities were wondering where their king had gone. Despite the current fragile state of the net, it wouldn't be hard to trace Arthur's path to West BI and now to the capital's spaceport. She fully expected someone to march up any minute and demand the king return to his duties.

When they arrived in Australia the situation would be no different. The country was a BA territory. If the government didn't catch up with him here, as soon as Arthur's ticket purchase registered in the system, someone would arrange to have personnel on the ground at their destination. He would be nabbed as soon as he disembarked. Hell, the government might force the shuttle to land in London.

The situation was kinda hopeless. She felt sorry for the king. He was obviously miserable in his new role. It had taken its toll on him already. White hairs had appeared in his red-golden mane and faint lines traced his features. But there was no way the BA would allow him to slip from their control. He was too valuable. He was in thrall to them just as much as he had been to Merlin.

Oh well.

She would let him live his dream for the short time it would take for his owners to catch up to him.

"Are you expecting someone?" asked Arthur, noticing her backward glances.

"No," she replied and gave him a tight smile.

"Something's bothering you."

"Yes, but I don't want to talk about it. What's been happening with you over the last couple of weeks?"

"Hm, like you, I don't particularly want to talk about it."

"That bad, huh?"

The line shuffled forward. Their credchips would be scanned for ID purposes when they reached the counter. That might be the moment the fantasy came to an end for Arthur. If it did, she hoped she wouldn't be prevented from boarding the shuttle too.

"Did you get to spend any time with Major Wright?" she asked.

"I did," Arthur replied, his features brightening.

She was pleased she'd hit on a mutually agreeable subject. She harbored fond memories of her kiss with the major before he left. If things had been different their relationship might have gone somewhere, but it was not to be.

"We had a few interesting chats," Arthur said, "but he had to leave. He wouldn't tell me where he was going. But the BA has been building a new spaceship, one capable of traveling between the stars. He seemed to have something to do with it."

"He wouldn't talk to you about it directly?"

"No. I don't think he could. They don't tell me the details. I'm only a face to them. An image or idea they use to meet their ends." His expression grew wistful. "In my time, when we went into battle, one man would carry the standard, a flag upon a high pole bearing our colors and symbols." The far-off look left his eyes and he continued, "To the Britannic Alliance, I am the battle standard and nothing more."

The line moved again, and Arthur stepped to the barrier, holding out his wrist to be scanned. But the check-in clerk wasn't interested in his wrist—she was eyeing his sword with alarm.

"Excuse me, sir, is that real?" She gestured at the weapon.

He seemed confused by the question. "Real?"

"Real or not," she said, "I'm afraid you can't bring it into the cabin. If you give it to me I'll arrange to have it put into the hold and it will be returned to you when you disembark."

It was a miracle they'd made it this far in the spaceport with the king's weapon hanging from his belt.

Arthur touched the hilt protectively. "I won't be parted from Excalibur."

"We have to consider the safety of the passengers and crew," the clerk reasoned. "You cannot board the shuttle carrying dangerous items, sir. It's against regulations."

It was a fair argument, and Arthur was a fair man—when he wasn't in his berserker rage, scything through human bodies like a farmer harvesting wheat. His brow furrowed. Maybe it wouldn't be the BI authorities swooping in and whisking him away that would put an end to his trip to Australia, maybe he would end the jaunt here himself by refusing to give up his sword.

To Taylan's amazement, he unbuckled his belt.

"Take good care of her," he said gravely, handing over the sword as if it was a newborn babe.

"Oh, we will, sir. We will." The clerk handled the weapon entirely differently, like a bomb, as she passed it to an assistant. She peered over the counter, her eyebrows raised. "You don't have any baggage?"

Taylan hadn't bothered to collect her few belongings from the house she'd been squatting in and Arthur apparently hadn't brought anything from London except Excalibur.

"No," she answered for both of them.

They had their chips scanned and they moved to the next section. No one had stepped forward to force Arthur to return to his duties.

And no one did step forward. Within half an hour, they were sitting side by side in the passenger cabin of the Sydney-bound shuttle. She scanned the ground, watching the crew loading the baggage, but no officials were madly scrambling to reach the spacecraft before it took off.

In another fifteen minutes, they were in the air.

The shuttle climbed rapidly to the upper atmosphere, the g-force pressing them into their seats. The surface of the planet rapidly receded. The horizon began to curve and the sky darkened.

She had never been able to afford to travel via shuttle. On rare trips abroad it had always been the slower, regular planes, jam-packed with other passengers, breathing stale air and eating shitty food. This new experience made a nice change. More importantly, she was finally on her way to find her kids. Arthur might be stopped in Sydney, but unless her terrorism charge had been re-instated, she would not. She was a free citizen. She allowed herself to imagine holding Patrin and Kayla again, and her eyes became wet.

"Thank you for doing this for me, Arthur."

"It's a pleasure to help a friend, and you are one of the few I have."

As he replied, his gaze was focused beyond her through the shuttle window.

"We're leaving the Earth behind," he remarked, peering downward.

"Yes, we'll fly through space for about half an hour."

Though Arthur had traveled in starships, he'd probably never actually seen space except as the night sky. As far as she knew, he'd never spacewalked and battle starships generally didn't have viewing portals as they weakened the ships' hulls.

She watched him as he saw the black for the first time, vicariously enjoying the wonder on his face. Then, while Arthur gazed out at the expanse wordlessly, she relaxed and closed her eyes.

What was the king's take on this new life he was leading? Did he still think it was a dream?

She began to doze. As she drifted off, she saw a battlefield where knights in armor on horses hacked at each other with swords. She faintly heard their cries. A standard flew above the battle, two long tails billowing in the breeze. Upon the flag a scaly red dragon writhed, its wings beating against a white background. The sounds of the battle grew louder: the clash of weapons, the screams of injured men, the roar of fighters calling to their comrades in arms.

A gust of wind blew, howling, and tore the flag from its pole. The material twisted and whirled, lifting high over the field before disappearing from sight among the clouds.

6

———

Taylan spied the delegation awaiting them at Sydney spaceport before they'd even disembarked. A huge crew of officials, police, and media reps was visible through the windows of the arrivals hall.

"Damn," she said softly.

"What's wrong?" Arthur asked.

She nodded in the direction of the hall. He peered through the shuttle window. It took him a minute to understand what she meant, but when he did he looked crestfallen. His small burst of freedom had come to an end.

"Is there another way out?" he asked.

"Nope, definitely not. We'll be corralled through the spaceport until we reach the arrivals area. Security is tight in places like this."

"Will I get Excalibur back before we meet them?"

Her jaw dropped. "You aren't thinking of fighting your way out?"

"Of course not. Those people haven't done me any harm. But I'm worried she won't be returned to me at all."

"Oh, you'll get her back at some point. I'm not sure when."

The Britannic Alliance wouldn't want him to be seen without his sword. It was as much a part of King Arthur's image as his mane of hair and beard.

"That's something, at least," he said sadly.

They waited while the other passengers disembarked. There was no point in hurrying the moment they would part company. Finally, everyone had departed. Taylan stepped out from her seat and they exited the shuttle.

"It's been pleasant spending time with you again," said Arthur as they walked along the spaceport passageway. "It's a shame our time together has been brief. Do you remember the time we journeyed through the West BI hills with T.J. and Merlin?"

"Absolutely."

What an odd experience it had been. She'd never seen Arthur so much in his element. The way he'd moved and behaved, as if he were a part of the ecosystem, it had been clear he was home at last.

"I would have liked to do some more trekking with you," he said.

"I don't think it would have been the same here. Australia's very different from West BI."

"How so?"

"For one thing, it's a lot hotter, especially in the area I'll be going, where Wright thought the Crusaders were taking the kids. A lot hotter and a lot drier. In West BI you're never far from water. In the outback you can easily die of dehydration if you aren't careful. The country's also way bigger than the Isles. You can't walk those distances."

Her heart sank as she remembered that, for her, these problems weren't hypothetical. She'd made it to Australia but she wasn't much better off than she'd been at home. She remained virtually penniless.

They passed through immigration smoothly. At the baggage

collection point, no one knew anything about Arthur's sword. Taylan began to fear she'd been wrong about him getting it back. The weapon was like a part of him. If it went missing he would be distraught. But then she noticed a spaceport official waiting at the exit, holding Excalibur in its scabbard awkwardly with two hands across his chest. A look of relief came over his anxious features when he spotted them.

Arthur marched up to him. "Thank you!"

Taylan waited as he fastened the belt. The king complete once more, they passed into Arrivals. The waiting crowd surged like the rising swell on an ocean. She had a brief sensation of being a world-famous celebrity, though it wasn't *her* everyone was here to see. She scanned the room, figuring out the best route to slip away unnoticed, and slowed her pace, allowing Arthur to draw ahead.

"Welcome to Australia, King Arthur!" said a woman in a smart skirt suit, moving forward from the throng. "We're so delighted to have you here, sir."

It was the Australian Prime Minister, Taylan realized with shock. She'd been expecting anonymous BA officials to orchestrate the public reception before whisking Arthur back to his duties.

Cameras were out all over the place and the king was looking like he would rather be anywhere than here. As he entered the melee, she began to sidle away from him, keeping her head down and her gaze averted as if she had nothing to do with him.

"You must be Taylan Ellis," said a voice.

She looked up at a uniform covering a broad male chest.

Shit.

Apparently, the Royal Marines operated in Australia too. Of course they did. Wright had been on duty here when he'd discovered the Crusaders' child trafficking.

There was no point in denying it. "Yes, I am. But," she added, "I'm not with the king. I'm traveling by myself."

Arthur had been swallowed by the throng.

"You're traveling alone?" the officer echoed. "That's strange. I was told to meet the two of you and help you prepare for your expedition."

"You were what?"

"There must have been a mistake. Never mind. Sorry to bother you."

He began to walk away.

She ran after him. "What did you say? You're supposed to help us?"

He paused and replied patiently, "My orders are to meet with the king after the official welcome, and someone called Taylan Ellis. That is you, right? I was sent your image."

"Yes, it's me. What was it you said about helping us prepare for our expedition?"

"The king is going to help with the search for the trafficked children. Are you working with him or not?"

Holy shit.

"I am! I mean, I will be working with him."

What was going on?

At some point in their two-hour trip over the globe, something had happened. Arthur's attempt to escape the BI government's clutches had transformed into a royal act of duty.

"Okay," said the Marine. "Come with me. The welcoming event should take about twenty minutes. When it's over we'll discuss your equipment requirements and give you a rundown on what we've done so far. You're booked on a transfer flight to Alice Springs."

Feeling like she was walking on air, she followed in the officer's wake as he forged a path through the crowd.

7

The compound was breaking up. In the darkness, beneath the camouflage canopy, the Crusaders were taking down tents, dismantling furniture, and transferring supplies to boxes and tubs. Gradually, the carts and wagons were filling up with everything portable. Other things, like the barn where the boy and his sister had slept all the months since they'd arrived and the high wooden surrounding fence, were to be destroyed.

No evidence is to be left behind, the boy had overheard.

Evidence of what?

The children who had died, he guessed, though their bones had to be somewhere out in the desert.

The children who had toiled and suffered and starved while people like Summoner Seba grew sleek and healthy.

It was funny. It didn't matter how much Seba ate or how good his food was, he was never happy or kind. If anything, eating better than most people in the compound seemed to make him angrier and more bitter. The boy grimaced.

"What's happening?" his sister asked.

The younger children had been herded into a group in the

center of the compound. The older ones were helping with packing up. While choosing who would help and who would wait, one of the organizers had hesitated over the boy. He'd bent his knees to look smaller and discourage her from picking him. It had worked. He wasn't sure if he'd done the right thing. He wasn't sure what would happen to the kids too young to help with heavy work. But he hadn't wanted to leave his sister. She was too small for most work. Who knew what might happen to her if—

"What's happening?" she repeated, tugging his sleeve.

"I think we're moving somewhere new."

"Why?"

"I don't know."

She huddled closer to him.

The people running the camp seemed scared and worried. They shouted and snapped at the children worse than ever, and they fumbled their own tasks, fear making them clumsy. They had to be preparing to go on the run. No fighter jets had passed overhead for a couple of weeks. No one had mentioned a word of it, but the Alliance must have won the war.

The compound had always been a secret place. In all his time here, the boy hadn't seen anyone make contact with the outside world. The Crusaders must have been hoping that one day everyone in the country would be a Crusader and they wouldn't have to hide anymore. But the opposite had happened, and now they had to move on before they were found out. Move on to where? And who would they take with them?

The boy still had nightmares about the dreadful trek from the boat to the road. They'd walked for kilometers through the hot, dry, empty land, only stopping briefly for water. If he hadn't carried his sister on his back the last part of the journey, he didn't think she would have made it.

Did they face the same trek again?

He was weaker now. They both were, and every vehicle would be full of equipment. The Crusaders would ride in them too, and there would be no room for anyone else. The children would have to walk. The boy didn't think many of them could walk for a whole day like they had before. He knew his sister couldn't.

"Hey!"

It was an urgent whisper.

A girl was slowly passing by, carrying a bundle of clothes. He knew her vaguely, though she belonged to a different section. Once, when they'd been gathering pumpkins, she'd offered to help him carry a large one but he hadn't agreed. He'd fallen and been beaten.

The girl's name was Hannah, though that couldn't be her real name.

"Don't wait," she said. "Run away, the first chance you get."

"What?" the boy asked stupidly. He'd understood what she'd said. He just couldn't take it in.

Checking around, she halted. "I just heard them say they have to kill the little ones or they'll slow us down."

"They…" Horror dried the words in his throat.

"I've told you what I know," said the girl. "It's up to you now."

She hastily moved on.

"They're gonna kill me?" asked his sister, her voice high and trembling.

Other children had heard Hannah's warning too. Ripples of shock and fear passed through the group as the words spread.

"No," the boy replied. "They're not gonna kill you."

"But that girl said—"

"They're not gonna kill you!"

He took her hand and gripped it so tight she winced, but she didn't ask him to let go.

His stomach churning, he looked around with new eyes.

Instead of watching the packing up, he looked for a way out. Activity surrounded them, Crusaders and older kids crossing to and fro. No one was paying them any attention, but if anyone tried to leave, they would be spotted quickly. Even worse, the fence remained standing. Until that had been dismantled or burned, the only exits were the two gates. They were open but carts and wagons were being driven through them regularly.

He had an idea.

Where had Hannah gone?

He searched the bustle until he found her. She was still carrying her bundle of clothes, but she was far away.

"Stay here," he said to his sister. "Don't move. I'll be back soon."

He could trust her to do as she was told. She was only small, but she was smart. She nodded at him, her eyes wide and teary.

He dashed from the group and dodged the men, women, handcarts, and piles of goods until he reached Hannah.

"What are you doing?" she whispered as he ran up.

He whispered his request but couldn't risk waiting for a reply before running back to his sister.

"Where are you going, you little bastard?" a man called out, aiming a kick at him as he ran past.

The boy was too fast. The man missed and, grumbling, went on his way. No one had time to mete out punishments. The ultimate punishment would come soon for the young kids anyway.

He made it back to his sister.

Most of the children were weeping, though some only stood in silence, their faces pale.

"It'll be all right," the boy told his sister, trying to reassure himself as much as her.

He watched the people. They didn't look at the waiting kids anymore, as if trying to prepare themselves for what was to come. Would Hannah do as he'd asked? Would she be able to?

A figure darted out and dropped something at the boy's feet, then she was gone.

Yes!

Hannah had done it.

He snatched the sack from the ground and shoved it under his shirt. The bulge made him look like he was going to have a baby, which was stupid, but no one was paying attention to him.

"What's that for?" his sister asked.

"You'll see."

He didn't think he was being ignored enough for no one to notice him doing something unusual, not even if he and his sister moved to the center of the group. If they were spotted, the adults might decide to put an end to the problem of the little children right away.

He clutched his belly, holding the sack tight, as he wondered what to do.

More wagons trundled through the two open gates. The camp was emptying. Less than half of it remained to be packed up. If he didn't move soon, it would be too late.

One of the horses hitched to a wagon snorted and reared. The boy glimpsed Hannah running away. She must have jabbed it or something. The horse bucked and jerked the wagon forward, dragging the other horse with it. Half-loaded contents spilled from the open back. There was an instant commotion as Crusaders ran to quieten the horse and reload the wagon.

The younger kids were completely ignored now.

Hannah had given him his chance.

He whipped the sack out from his shirt and opened the top. "Quick, hop in," he told his sister.

Without hesitating or asking why, she jumped right in it. He closed the top and hoisted her over his shoulder. Before leaving he turned to the other kids and said, "Run! Try to get out!"

The group broke and scattered.

This caused more disturbance. The Crusaders quickly saw what was going on and tried to catch the little kids. The boy wasn't the first focus of their attention because he was carrying a sack. He looked like he was helping with the packing up.

He walked confidently, like he knew where he was going.

He *did* know where he was going. He was heading for the north gate.

The horse Hannah had spooked was quiet now, but the running children continued to cause mayhem. Some were recaptured and carried away, struggling. Some of the bigger ones climbed onto wagons. The boy guessed their idea was to hide among the supplies. They might be lucky and get away with it, but *he* wasn't going to risk being caught and killed on the journey.

He began to speed up. The commotion was dying down.

He was only a few meters from the gate when someone stepped into his path. He almost walked right into her. He looked up at the Crusader woman, who was staring down at him suspiciously.

"Where are you going? The grain is to go on Seba's wagon."

"I, uh... He told me to put it on that one." The boy jerked his chin at the cart nearest the north gate.

"Hm. Wait here." She strode off.

He waited, watching her. When she was ten paces away, she looked back. They always did that. They never trusted you to do as you were told.

As soon as she turned her head again, he ran.

His arms were already aching and the rough fabric of the sack felt like it was scraping his skin off, but he only had to make it as far as—

"Hey, stop!" It was the woman. She must have checked on him for a second time.

A wagon was about to pass through the gate. He sped to the other side of it, where he would be hidden from searching eyes.

"Stop that kid! Darn it. Where's he gone?"

Crouching down, he kept pace with the creaking wheels.

In another second, he was through the gate. He flew into the darkness, his sister bumping on his back. Gasping, stumbling he ran through the desert scrub. The night air was cold in his lungs as they heaved. He ran as far as he could before collapsing. The sack slipped from between his fingers and he lay on his back, catching his breath.

Kayla climbed out of the sack and crawled over to him.

"Thank you for saving me, Patrin."

She remembered his name! For months, she'd been calling him the hated name the Crusaders had given him.

He sat up, picked up the sack, and wrapped it around both their shoulders.

In the distance, the compound lanterns shone out, the only lights at ground level. Above them hung the bright starscape.

Patrin watched and listened for several minutes.

No one seemed to have come out of the compound to search for them. The Crusaders probably didn't want to waste the effort and time. It was hard to survive alone out here without food or water. They probably figured any kids who escaped would die soon anyway.

The wagons slowly pulled away down a track that led into the desert. Before they got far, all that was visible of them was the swaying beams of their lamps. Then more lights appeared: licking tongues of flame. Someone had set light to the camouflage canopy and the fence.

The children slipped away into the night.

8

Taylan couldn't believe her luck. Not only was she going to be fully equipped for her search in the inhospitable Australian outback, no one was going to come after her trying to find an AWOL king.

What had Hans Jonte told the BI Government? How had he spun Arthur running away from his duties to them? Somehow, Jonte made everything okay. Maybe he'd pointed out that unless they made Arthur's life more bearable, they might lose him entirely. They were relying on the monarch's cooperation. If he refused to give speeches or attend events they couldn't force him.

Maybe Jonte had encouraged them to take pity on him. After all, anyone who spent more than thirty seconds in Kala Orr's company would sympathize with Arthur's plight.

"You'll be going off road," said the Royal Marine officer assigned to help their preparations, a woman called Pappadopoulos, "which means you'll be out of reach of the net and driving yourself. It isn't too hard once you get the hang of it."

She was talking about the all-terrain vehicle the Australian Search-and-Rescue Division was lending them.

Taylan glanced at Arthur. *She* would have to do all the driving. The king could barely operate a comm button, and that was a recent accomplishment since overcoming his fear of them.

"I'm sure I'll figure it out," she told Pappadopoulos.

"I'm sure you will." She went on to list the equipment already loaded, including a water condensing device for drawing moisture from the atmosphere. "It won't make enough to supply all your needs. The air's dry as a bone out there. But the map in your vehicle's database shows all the known water sources. Just be careful you don't run too low before you stock up. Which brings me to the sanitizer. Don't drink any ground water or use it for cooking until you've run it through that."

"How long will the vehicle battery last?" asked Taylan, concerned they might not be able to search for very long. There would be no recharge stations in the bush.

"Years," Pappadopoulos replied.

In response to Taylan's raised eyebrows, she explained, "They've finally figured out how to make fusion cells small enough for motor vehicles. The Search-and-Rescue fleet is fitted with some of the first cells off the production line. They've passed the safety checks, but as with all new tech, there's a higher chance of failure. So that's another thing to watch out for. The computer will tell you if it senses anything going wonky. If that happens, don't ignore it. Comm us." A pained expression appeared on her face. "I don't want to have to send out a team to rescue you too. We're already flat out looking for those kids."

"Got it," Taylan said. "I'll keep an eye on the dash." The last thing she wanted to do was to divert the people who were looking for her children.

"Good. Right, let me show you the areas already searched.

The local police forces and army reservists are looking too. The effort so far has focused on working inland from the coast, but there's still a whole lot of ground to cover. We have a suggestion on where you should try. You'll be approaching the area from the west."

FOUR HOURS LATER, Taylan and Arthur were in their vehicle, deep within the Australian desert. Darkness was falling swiftly. Pappadopoulos had cautioned against driving at night, explaining there was a good chance of crashing into a kangaroo.

"Not that the 'roo would be a match for your bull bar," she'd said, "but it'll be bloody and messy and you won't like it."

Taylan braked, bringing the car to a halt, and turned off the engine. There was no need to search for a flat, dry, open piece of ground as she would have in West BI. Just about everywhere in the outback was flat and dry and the vegetation grew sparsely. There was also no danger of another vehicle crashing into them. They'd left the road a couple of hours ago.

She pressed the button to release the camper extension.

The king had been silent for most of their journey, gazing out at the barren landscape. What did he make of it all? Was he trying to square what he was seeing with tales of unknown lands from his previous life? Was he imagining a blank part of a map stating *Here be dragons*? Or was his Dark Ages' mind simply unable to process the view and he was more like a computer failing to boot?

"Time to eat and sleep," she said. "I want to leave at first light tomorrow."

Her words pulled him from his trance. He opened the door. "I'll look for wood."

"We don't need to make a fire. We have self-warming food and a heater for when it gets cold later."

"Self-cooking food?" He didn't seem to like the idea.

As it turned out, his foreboding was spot on. The rations that heated themselves when you pulled out a tab tasted disgusting. Taylan had some kind of pasta mush and Arthur had picked a stew. Screwing up their faces after their first tastes, they tried each other's meals and discovered each tasted the same kind of bad.

The heater gave a better result. The desert night chill had already begun to invade the tent by the time they finished eating and were bedding down. The minute Taylan turned the heater on, warm air filled the tent. She checked the water condenser was working and then unrolled her sleeping bag.

Arthur was sitting on his bag already, getting undressed. He pulled off his shirt, revealing the tattoo that ran across his chest, just below his collar bones. She'd always meant to ask him about his tattoos.

"It shows a hunt," he said, noticing her interest. "The lion is chasing deer and he's about to catch one. Can you see?"

She peered closer. Now he'd pointed it out, she could make out the figure leaping higher than the deer was indeed a stylized lion.

"It gives me strength and courage."

"The tattoo?"

He nodded and turned. "The ones on my back are magical symbols to protect me from evil."

"Cool. I have some tatts as well, though they don't do anything magical. They're just things close to my heart."

"You have? Can I see them?"

Taylan pushed her sleeves up to her shoulders. The names Patrin and Kayla curled over one of her biceps. "My kids' names," she explained. On her other arm were the words

Cymru am byth. "It means *Long live West BI*. Cymru is the real name for my country."

"Our country," Arthur corrected, pulling off his boots.

She'd managed to persuade him to stow his sword with the rest of the equipment in the back of the vehicle.

"Yes," she said, "our country."

"Your name for it sounds similar to mine. It must be a very old word now."

"Yeah, must be." She also took off her boots and placed them at the end of her sleeping bag before unzipping it.

Her mind turned to tomorrow, when the search for her kids would begin. They were in a part of the Northern Territory the Search-and-Rescue team hadn't managed to cover yet. Satellite imagery and scans had turned up no sign of the Crusaders, so the team members were scouring the ground with helis and vehicles square kilometer by square kilometer. Australia was damned big.

No one was sure exactly what they were looking for, though Pappadopoulos had said the Crusaders must have some kind of camp and they had to be doing something to screen it from observation. The ships used to bring the kids in had cloths overhanging them, and it was likely the camps had something similar that would make them hard to see from a distance. But there were signs to look for, signs of activity like worn tracks. Pappadopoulos had also said she doubted the Crusaders were shipping in their food. The group Wright had followed from the coast hadn't been carrying many supplies. That could mean the Crusaders were growing crops. Few plants would survive in the desert, but in the northern regions the climate was wetter and the ground more fertile.

Taylan planned on driving north tomorrow heading for an area that straddled the desert and the greener region.

Seeing that Arthur had lain down and was ready to sleep, she turned out the light.

"You're proud of our country, aren't you, Taylan?" he asked softly in the darkness.

"Of course I am. Aren't you?"

"Naturally, but it's good to hear you say it. You were born thousands of years after me, but your pride remains true to the land I fought for." He paused then said, "Many things have been weighing heavily on my mind since I discovered Merlin's trickery."

"Like what?"

"In my former life, I committed many great sins. I killed many people, praying for forgiveness every time. Merlin assured me I would have that forgiveness, that what I was doing was necessary to prevent more suffering and to protect my people. When I learned he only told me that because he was playing me like a piece in a game of chess, it shook me. I have committed the sin of murder at his bidding. He didn't know if I will be forgiven or if when I die my soul will achieve rest. He lied."

As he went on, his tone was quiet and fearful. "I am damned Taylan. Damned for all eternity. Yet, when I see your love for the country I killed so many people to defend, it gives me some solace."

She didn't know how to answer him. She wasn't religious, and even if she were, what he was saying was true. He *had* killed hundreds if not thousands of people. Murder *was* a sin according to his faith. Merlin *had* lied.

All she could think to answer was, "I do love my country, Arthur. I'm proud of it and always will be. The same goes for my countrymen and women. You might have killed a lot of people, but you did great good in your life, and your legacy has passed down through the ages. No matter what happens when you die, that'll always be true."

He was silent for so long she thought he must have gone to

sleep, but then he said, "You're like your forebear, Lancelot. He always knew what to say to give me comfort too."

Taylan had been drifting off. At first, she struggled to make sense of his words. She mumbled, "I'm glad I could…"

His meaning filtered through, and her eyes snapped open.

Then she decided she must have misheard. "Ha, for a minute there I thought you said my forebear Lancelot."

"I did say that."

She lifted herself on one elbow and turned to face Arthur, though he was invisible in the pitch black. "Lancelot was my ancestor? You're joking, right?"

"No. Why would I joke about it?"

"How could you…? I mean, I don't doubt he existed, but you can't possibly know I'm descended from him."

"But I do. Some things you just know. You fight exactly like him. Merlin saw it too, that day when we sparred on the *Fearless* and I broke your nose. He agreed with me, though he probably knows more about it than I do."

She flopped onto her back. She was descended from Sir Lancelot of the Round Table? She was delighted by the idea. Dad would have been ecstatic. If what Arthur was saying was true, it had to have been her father who had passed on the ancient knight's genes.

"You should know," Arthur added, "Merlin made Lancelot a great fighter by casting spells on him. You have inherited them."

9

———

A sea of baking red soil and rocks spread out in all directions under a clear azure sky. Heat hung over the desert in a shimmering haze, and the sun was a blurred, glaring circle of white-yellow.

They'd been traveling north-east for five hours after setting out before dawn. The air had been frigid then. Now, their vehicle's dashboard displayed an outside temperature of 45 C, predicted to reach 48. Taylan recalled Wright saying how he and Abacha had been forced to turn back when following the Crusader child traffickers. At the time, she'd been distraught, wondering how he could have abandoned the trail before finding out where the kids were being taken. Seeing the temperature and landscape for herself, she understood a little better. No one would last long here without water or shade.

The understanding brought her little comfort, however. The conditions Wright had found unbearable were the same ones Patrin and Kayla had been enduring. Though they might have water and food, they weren't fully grown men like Wright and Abacha. They were young and weak.

Assuming they were still alive.

Her breath caught in her throat, and their vehicle swerved slightly, clipping a thorn bush.

Arthur laid a hand on her arm. "Maybe you should take a break."

"Not yet. I can manage another hour."

A break from driving would have been good. It hadn't been hard to learn how to guide the vehicle—the pedals were basically 'go' and 'stop', and there was nothing substantial around for her to hit—but it was hard work. She was used to inputting a destination and letting the car take her there. Here in the outback she had to navigate every rock and bush, and the distances were so great the dot representing them on the map crawled along frustratingly slowly.

Her arms and neck ached. The tinted windshield protected her eyes from the sun's glare, but they were tired from concentrating on the ground ahead.

"Did you think any more about what I told you last night?" Arthur asked.

"You mean about me being descended from Lancelot? I thought about it. It's a nice idea, but when you think about it, though I suppose it might be true, it isn't remarkable. It's been thousands of years since Lancelot died. You both lived so long ago, hundreds of thousands of people must be related to him and to you. Except..."

Whoops.

Too late for her brain to catch up with her mouth, she'd remembered parts of the Arthur legend that told her no one was descended from him. She'd strayed onto a sensitive subject.

"Sorry," she said lamely.

Speaking quietly, he asked, "So the story of my marriage made it down the ages too?"

"Yes, it did. Well, *a* story did. I don't know how much of it really happened."

"I never sired any children with my wife. She was barren."

"It wasn't necessarily her fault. I mean, I know you had Mordred with Morgan, but that doesn't mean your later problem was all your wife's. Fertility is complicated."

"Marriages are complicated too."

She couldn't look at him, remembering the other parts of the story of Arthur, Guinevere, and Lancelot. Somehow, she felt responsible for the actions of her supposed long-distant ancestor, as if it was up to *her* to explain why his best friend had an affair with his wife. Although it was all literally ancient history, to Arthur these were events of the recent past. The fact that even the bones of the people involved were dust now didn't matter.

"I'm sorry about what happened," she said.

He sighed. "So were they."

After a while, he went on, "But what I told you before is correct. I'm certain of it. I admit I know little about human fertility, but I see the evidence of Merlin's spells in you, and his spells never failed. The passage of time was no impediment to him."

"Maybe I just can't quite believe it. I grew up hearing stories about you two and other knights, but I never imagined *I* might become a part of the story." She continued curiously, "Did Merlin used to cast spells on you too? I've seen you fight, and it's like you're another person."

"Yes, I was besmirched with his magic just as much as you are."

His reply brought her some reassurance. Twice, he'd come close to killing her while in his fighting rage. "So now Merlin isn't around anymore, are you vulnerable to pulse fire?"

"If you mean the lights fired by your weapons, I don't know. I have never been fired upon without Merlin present."

She spared a moment from concentrating on driving to glance at him. Over the last couple of days she'd confirmed her first impression of him when he'd come to see her in prison. He definitely looked older. "And how do you feel? I mean generally speaking."

"You've noticed I am aging too? I feel tired in body and soul. I think when Merlin dissolved and went away, he removed his protection from me."

"Cutting off his head probably annoyed him."

Arthur chuckled. "Probably. But it felt good at the time."

She drove on for another hour, until her shoulder and arm muscles were cramped and sore. It was impossible to go twenty meters without encountering an object to be avoided, and though the vehicle's suspension provided a buffer between their backsides and the rocky ground, it didn't offer full protection.

She drew to a halt. "Let's eat."

While Arthur was finding selections different from last night's dinner, she broke out the drones. They weren't near their chosen search area yet, but it wouldn't hurt to practice with the surveillance devices. She'd seen them deployed while working as a Marine but they'd never been her responsibility.

When used in combat, their feeds were relayed to the relevant officer's HUD. For search-and-rescue purposes, the telemetry the drones captured was displayed on the vehicle's dash. Taylan picked ten of the marble-sized drones from the box, activated them, and threw them into the air. Their default behavior was to spread themselves out, divide up the immediate area equally, and begin scanning it. As soon as they'd finished surveying the section they would spread out farther. The process continued until they were recalled or ran out of juice. Survi-drones were good for spotting enemy soldiers in broad daylight, until anti-drone devices took them out at least, but at night the infrared dampening of combat armor made them less useful.

Taylan slid into the driver's seat and turned on the interface. The computer had already begun compiling the drones' data into one bird's eye image. The vehicle sat in the center surrounded by the harsh desert landscape she'd been seeing for the past day and a half. Detailed figures relating to ground temperature, air temperature, wind speed and other local conditions stood in a line in a corner of the screen, drawn from the drone's sensors.

"These are to be eaten cold," said Arthur, passing her a package through her open window.

When he took his seat, she closed both windows and turned on the aircon. The foil-covered packet he'd handed her was thick and square. She peeled it open, revealing a sandwich. She sniffed it.

"Is something wrong?" Arthur asked.

"These rations are good for..." she checked the date "...three years. How can they make a sandwich last three years?"

"You're asking the wrong person. In my time, bread was eaten the day it was made."

She took a bite. The meat filling wasn't identifiable, but it tasted better than last night's pasta and that was good enough.

One eye on the gradually widening image displayed on the interface, she asked, "What was it you were telling me about Major Wright and the BA's new starship?" Using the drones had reminded her of the major.

"I think I told you as much as I know, which is very little. The ship is to be called the *Dauntless*, and it will travel to other suns. I believe TJ is to go with it."

"I wonder why."

"Why what?"

"Why the BA wants to leave the solar system. I know why Wright's going. He's following orders, the same as always."

"I'm not sure. There was a man at the meetings who seemed

to have some authority though he wasn't military. A red-headed man I'd met before aboard the *Gallant*."

A red-headed man involved with an interstellar mission?

"Do you remember his name?"

"I remember it was odd. Most people I meet, if they aren't a military officer, are introduced as Mr or Ms. But he wasn't. I think his first name began with an L."

"Was it Lorcan? Lorcan Ua Talman?"

"Yes, that's it. Do you know him?"

"Everyone knows him. He's been building three colony ships for about twenty years. That makes a lot of sense. He must be helping the Alliance build an FTL engine."

"FTL?"

"Faster than light."

Arthur burst into laughter. "Light doesn't travel. It exists or it doesn't. What a strange notion."

"You need to go to school."

Still laughing, he conceded, "Maybe I do."

Taylan was pleased he seemed happy. It was a big improvement from how he'd been when he'd walked into her prison cell just a few days ago. But then, *she* felt a lot better too.

She finished the last of her sandwich. "Let's go."

It was time to recall the drones. She peered at the screen a final time to check she hadn't missed anything. They were still far from the intended search area, but it wouldn't hurt to look. The devices had covered about a square kilometer in the time they'd been eating, and their vehicle was now a dot in the dusty red wilderness on the screen. It wasn't possible to make out any detail at the current scale so she halted the data input and segmented the image into squares before looking at each in turn.

Red desert, patch of scrub, rock, hole, another rock, a rotting kangaroo carcass, a third rock, more desert, a fourth—

Arthur, who had also been peering at the screen, touched her hand. "Do you see it?"

"Uhh..."

His finger traced a line on the image. She bent closer and squinted. She still could see nothing except dry sand.

"It's a track," he said.

10

The sun was a furnace blazing against Taylan's back as she squatted in the dust. Now she was about half a meter away from them, she could finally clearly see the uniform lines in the soil Arthur had spotted so easily on the interface screen. The man seemed to have different eyes than hers—than most people, she guessed.

Very faint, zigzagging tire marks filled the gap between the two, marginally less faint, lines that formed the edges of the track.

Arthur was wandering around, peering down.

"What are you looking for?" she asked.

"The other track."

She straightened up. "You mean from other tires?"

"Yes. Vehicles have four wheels so there should be two sets of tracks, but I can only see one."

She began to search the red dust too. The marks Arthur had identified ran through a thin layer of soil on hard, flat rock. Everywhere else, the rock was harder and the soil sparser. And a hot, gusty wind was blowing, which could have simply blown away all other evidence of a vehicle passing this way.

"Can you tell how old this one is?" she asked.

"When was the last time it rained?"

"I'd have to check, but I'd guess it hasn't rained out here in weeks."

"Then the track could be a day or weeks old."

She didn't know what to make of it.

Arthur walked away, continuing to scan the ground.

She decided to let him do his thing and not distract him. She returned to the vehicle to get out of the sun and to check the recent weather reports. Inside the cool interior, she discovered the last time it had rained in this area was four years ago. Could the track be *that* old?

It probably didn't mean anything. They were far from the regions where farming was possible. Far from anywhere in fact. She couldn't imagine even Crusaders with their back-to-basics way of life persisting here for long.

She watched Arthur wander a few tens of meters across the rust-colored landscape before he returned, flushed and sweating. A blast of warm air hit her as he climbed into the vehicle.

"Did you find the second track?"

He shook his head. "Do some of your vehicles only have two wheels?"

"Yes. Well, some used to. We used to have motorbikes, but they've been illegal since before I was born."

"Then it was a motorbike that passed this way."

She told him what she'd found out about the last time rain fell.

"The tracks aren't years old," he said. "The wind would erase them in that time. I would say they were made between a couple of days and two or three weeks ago. It isn't very accurate, but that's the best I can do."

"Your best is pretty good. I couldn't even see those marks until I was right on top of them. Still, I think there's no point in following them. Whoever passed through here, I don't think he or she is anything to do with the Crusaders. One, they can't farm out here, and, two, motorized transportation isn't their style."

In her time living among them, she had learned that although Crusaders would sometimes use engine-driven vehicles for expediency's sake, they would avoid them if they could. She imagined the group forging a life in the wilderness to prepare for their Dwyr's invasion were probably fundamentalists. They would be even less likely to be riding motorbikes around the place.

"I disagree," said Arthur. "I think we should follow the track and find out who made it."

"But why? We should be searching in more likely areas than this. Following a random trail is a waste of time. There could be hundreds of them crossing the desert."

"There aren't hundreds. This is the first one we've seen since we left the road."

"But I only put up the drones just now."

"I've been looking all the time you've been driving. This is the first sign of another human being we've encountered."

"Okay," she replied, somewhat abashed. She'd assumed Arthur had been mindlessly staring out the windows the whole time. "But it still doesn't mean anything. We can't go chasing after every small thing we see. We don't have time." Her throat had tightened as she spoke.

It was the landscape that did it. Ever since she'd seen it first hand, the impossibility of anyone surviving long out here struck her more deeply each passing hour.

He laid a hand on her arm. "If Merlin were here, he would say to follow it. He would say it was no coincidence we stopped in this place to eat, or that you chose to send up the drones, or that I happened to see that track."

"You're not exactly selling it, you know, telling me what

Merlin, of all people, would think. He sounds like a bloody Crusader."

"He understands these things far better than us. He would say it was a pattern, and we should follow where the pattern leads us."

"Well the pattern he followed led to him having his head chopped off. I wonder what he thought about that?"

Arthur smiled. "He didn't like it, I'm sure." His expression turned serious. "I don't know how to convince you, but I believe strongly we should follow the trail."

There was something in the earnestness of his look that persuaded her. It was the old Arthur back again, the one she recognized from the first time she'd come to know him on the *Valiant*, before she'd seen him mercilessly slaughter helpless men and women.

"Okay." She started the engine. "I hope you're right."

Five hours later, they were no wiser about who they were following or what the person was doing. The motorbike tracks —it had to be a motorbike, they hadn't discovered a parallel line anywhere—led them on a meandering route through the desert. Their progress was painfully slow as Arthur insisted on stopping often to inspect the marks more closely, checking for signs of freshness and the rider's other activities. Whoever it was, he or she had halted every few kilometers, walked away from their bike, and dug in the dirt.

Taylan hadn't been able to figure out what they were doing, and she'd reach the end of her tether. She was exhausted and frustrated.

Evening had arrived, and the sun disappeared like a candle blown out.

She braked hard, jerking herself and Arthur forward in their seats. "That's enough for today. Tomorrow, we head north."

"But we—"

"No. We stop here. At first light, we return to the original plan. We've wasted enough time on this wild goose chase." She opened her door and got out.

"But we aren't chasing a—"

She slammed the door shut.

We have to go where the pattern leads us, she mimicked bitterly in her head. *It's what Merlin would have done.*

Damned Dark Ages throwback.

Arthur emerged. "You forgot to create the tent."

Scowling, she jerked her door open and pressed the relevant button. The back of the vehicle popped out to form the tent. All they had to do was secure it to the ground. The king started on the task while she stretched her aching back and arms.

The change in position began to ease her frustration. She joined Arthur to push the pegs into the soil. "Sorry for snapping at you, but we need to focus on what we came here to do, which is find my kids."

"If you say so," he replied mildly. "Perhaps I was wrong."

From his tone, however, it was clear he didn't think he was mistaken.

Whatever.

She'd done the right thing and taken his input seriously, but surely even he had to admit now they were no further on in finding the Crusaders? The old king might be a fantastic tracker, but he was not of this time. His understanding of the modern world was poor. She would have to politely ignore what he had to say from now on.

11

It was roughly two in the morning when they heard the motorbike. Arthur had heard the engine noise first and woke Taylan. As she came to, the whine was the first thing to reach her consciousness after registering Arthur shaking her shoulder. The sound was soft and far distant but unmistakably artificial compared to the nocturnal desert noises.

"We have to follow it," said the king.

"Do we?" she asked sleepily. "I thought we agreed it's a waste of time."

"We didn't agree. You decided."

"All right, but there's no way that's a Crusader. So I can't see any point—"

"We have to follow it," Arthur repeated.

His movement had caused the tent light to activate, and in its glow she saw the intensity of his look.

"Okay," she said wearily.

Minutes later, the tent was packed up, their bags and other paraphernalia hastily jammed into the back of the vehicle, and she was in the driver's seat. As she started up the engine, the stupidity of what they were trying to do hit her. "It won't work. How are we going to hear the motorbike over our own vehicle's noise?"

Their engine wasn't loud, but it was loud enough to mask sound from their surroundings.

Arthur lowered his window. "Can you hear it now?"

"Not really."

He gave her a quizzical look and then leaned out, hanging an arm over the door. "Drive. I'll tell you where to go."

The night vision display lit up on the windscreen. She was used to night vision on a HUD, yet the difference from a regular sunlit landscape still slowed her down. Coupled with the necessity of navigating the rocky and vegetative obstacles, they barely made 20 K an hour. A motorbike could move much faster, but the rider might not be trying to get away from them. They know they were being followed yet.

She drove on, guided by Arthur's pointing finger.

An occasional startled animal leapt from their path, eyes glowing like a demon's in the night vision. The desert seemed to come to life at night. She hadn't noticed so many creatures during the daytime. Perhaps they were too well-camouflaged.

Arthur shook his head. "The motorbike is getting away from us."

"I can't go any faster."

He leaned back in his seat, appearing to give up.

She eased off the accelerator. "It probably doesn't matter anyway."

Arthur was frowning. He clearly didn't agree.

"Look" she said, "if that motorbike rider is 'part of the pattern' as you say, us catching up to him should be part of the pattern too, shouldn't it? It doesn't make any sense otherwise."

She braked to a stop and turned off the engine. The night vision display disappeared, and Arthur sat suddenly sat upright. "There he is!"

In the distance, a faint beam of light moved at ground level in the darkness. A headlight.

"Yeah," said Taylan, tired and irritated, "but—"

"Drive that way," said Arthur, pointing again.

She could see what he meant. If they went in the new direction they would cut the motorbike off.

"Arthur, this is pointless."

"Taylan, please drive."

Sighing, she started up the engine. She would humor him for now, but tomorrow she would have to put her foot down.

The king was looking out the side window again, tracking the beam of light. Their vehicle had no headlights but as its path converged with the bike's, the rider would be more likely to hear it, if not the engine, then their passage through the brush.

She could see the headlight beam clearly now too. The shaft of light ran at an angle to them, not deviating. The rider hadn't noticed them.

"Slow down," said Arthur.

She complied.

How come their quarry hadn't noticed the large search-and-rescue vehicle only fifty or so meters away? She guessed meeting another vehicle in the desert had to be the last thing on the rider's mind. She drove slowly forward, no longer needing the king's guidance on blocking the motorcycle's path. If she did manage it, she hoped the rider didn't get hurt in the collision.

Another few meters and the headlight was shining directly into their side windows.

Surely they were obvious now?

"He's going to hit us!" Arthur exclaimed.

Taylan thought so too and moved to press the accelerator, but at the last instant, the light swerved.

She watched the motorcyclist speed past, catching a

glimpse of a helmeted, rangy male figure riding it. Then the bike was gone.

WHEN SHE WOKE the following morning, she groaned from lack of sleep. Determined to not pay attention to Arthur's uninformed suggestions anymore, she didn't speak to him as she dug out some breakfast for them.

After they'd given up the chase and set up camp he hadn't mentioned anything about the night's escapade, and he didn't after they woke up. He seemed unembarrassed and unfazed. She fully expected him to go out and begin tracking the mysterious motorbike again.

They ate in silence. She chewed her cereal bar sourly.

A part of her knew her mood was also due to her fear and worry over Patrin and Kayla. It was easier to be angry at her friend than it was to contemplate what might have happened to her kids. But another part of her was genuinely pissed off at the ancient king, who seemed intent on gallivanting around the desert rather than getting down to the real and hard work of tracking down the Crusaders.

"Finished?" she asked, standing and holding out her hand for his wrappers.

He handed them over and she stuffed them in the garbage bag.

She checked the condenser. It had filled only halfway overnight. She emptied the water into their main container.

"Ready?" she asked.

The king nodded in answer and unfastened the tent door. She followed him into the sunlight, searingly bright after the darkness of the tent.

"Just to be clear," she said, "we're back to our original plan today, right?"

"The original plan?"

"Yes," she said patiently, "we're driving the rest of the way to the borderlands, remember?"

"You don't want to find the motorbike rider?"

"No. As we discovered last night, it's hopeless trying to catch him. His vehicle is faster and more maneuverable than ours in this terrain. And it's obvious he doesn't want to meet us or he would have stopped when he nearly ran into our vehicle."

"We must have surprised him, suddenly appearing in his path."

"He still could have stopped, but he didn't. We can't catch him if he doesn't want to be caught, and even if we could, there's absolutely no guarantee he can help us anyway."

Arthur shrugged. "If you say so, only—"

"I do say so. I'm glad we're on the same page. Help me pack up the tent and we'll leave right away. If we make good time we might reach our destination tonight."

Ignoring what she'd said, the king continued, "...only my guess is there's a good chance our motorbike rider is over there." He indicated a distant clump of trees with a nod.

"What?" she asked. "Where?" She shaded her eyes with her hand and squinted at the trees, which stood a few hundred meters distant. She couldn't see anything resembling a motorbike. "What makes you think he's there?"

"He needs water. He won't be able to carry very much on his bike and he doesn't have room for the machine that creates it from the air. If I were him, I would have camped there overnight."

"But how do you know that place has water?" She hadn't noticed him studying their map. She wasn't even sure he could read it properly.

He frowned at her. "Can't you see those trees are taller and stronger and different from all the others around us? Really, Taylan, sometimes it's like you're blind as well as deaf."

12

"What are you doing?" Taylan asked.

Arthur was rummaging around in the back of their vehicle. They were going to approach the clump of trees he'd spotted on foot. If they drove over there, the noise of their engine might spook the motorcyclist and, as they'd discovered last night, once he was on his bike they would never catch him.

Arthur was on his tiptoes, his upper half hidden among their stacked equipment and supplies. When he emerged, grinning, he was holding his sword in its scabbard.

"No!" she exclaimed. "No way. We were talking about not frightening him. How do you think he's going to react if he sees you waving that around?"

"But he might be dangerous."

"Pappadopoulos gave us both sidearms. We can use those if we have to."

"I'm not comfortable with your weapons."

This was true. They'd done a little target practice but Arthur's aim was wild. When she'd suggested imagining the pulse round was an arrow he'd been better, but he clearly wasn't comfortable firing a gun.

"That can't be helped," she said. "Don't worry. It's only one guy. If he gets jumpy I can deal with him."

"But Excalibur goes everywhere with me."

"Arthur, please. Trust me on this. I trusted you and followed the pattern you claimed to see, didn't I?"

Giving her a sulky glance, he wordlessly slid the sword back among their belongings.

"We need hats," she said. "Can you get them out?"

The sun was already warming the air as they walked toward the trees. Reddish-brown earth dotted with dusky green scrub spread out to the encircling horizon and cobalt sky. The trees they were heading for *were* taller and greener than the rest of the vegetation, she realized as she studied them more closely. Why had it taken Arthur pointing them out for her to notice?

As they neared the clump, the king began throwing her annoyed looks. After the third or fourth glance, he put a hand on her shoulder and whispered, "Tread more softly. You sound like a stallion after a mare in heat."

She quietened her footsteps as well as she could, but she could tell from Arthur's expression he wasn't satisfied. Eventually, his broad hand came down on her shoulder again.

"Wait here," he said quietly. "I will catch him."

"Okay, but don't hurt him."

There was no reason to believe the man roaming the outback on his motorbike had anything to do with the Crusader traffickers. She hadn't been able to figure out what the hell he *was* doing out here while apparently aimlessly wandering the desert, stopping every so often to dig in the dirt, but it wasn't necessarily anything illegal.

She waited, hands on hips, as Arthur closed the remaining distance alone.

He entered the trees where they grew most thickly. The

main group stood fifty to sixty meters wide. The line petered out to the west, stretching another hundred meters or so. The water supplying the trees' roots had to flow along the line until it dried out or ran too deep for the roots to reach.

It was obvious now she thought about it. She realized at home in West BI, she sometimes read the landscape as Arthur did, only water was not in short supply there. But she knew that trees growing on a hill meant the slope was too steep for sheep to graze, allowing the trees to flourish.

Arthur re-emerged from the undergrowth and beckoned her.

She walked over, trying to avoid crunching the soil beneath her feet.

When she reached him, he whispered in her ear, "The man is asleep, but he has many strange items of machinery. I didn't know if any of them are dangerous."

She followed him between the trunks until he gestured for her to get down. They crawled the last few paces. He indicated a narrow gap in the undergrowth and moved out of her way so she could take a peek.

A pool of clear water lay in a clearing, reflecting the tree canopy in its still surface. The motorbike was the second thing she noticed. An old model, of course. To her knowledge, no company had produced motorbikes for decades. This machine showed its age, thick with scratches and dust, the seat squashed and frayed. But despite its aged state, their experience had shown it was a better vehicle for getting around the outback than their bulky four-wheel-drive.

What was more perplexing was the array of 'machinery' that had set Arthur on edge. She only recognized one item: a solar sheet for charging the bike's battery lay in a patch of sunlight. The three other pieces of equipment were unfamiliar. Metal boxes with interface displays on the outside, they could be anything. Yet they didn't look dangerous.

She was about to whisper her assessment to Arthur when the sleeping man began to stir. He was lying on his back, his head hidden behind one of his bike's wheels.

She drew back into the shadow of the low vegetation.

Now was the time to grab the man, before he was out of his sleeping bag and better able to move around.

I think it's safe, she mouthed to Arthur.

He nodded.

She pointed at his chest and then to a spot on the opposite side of their quarry. Arthur set off for the place she'd indicated. He would approach the man from the other side of the clearing after moving through the undergrowth more quietly than she could manage.

The legs in the sleeping bag moved again.

Damn!

The man was waking up.

The sound of a zipper being drawn broke the hush.

Where was Arthur? Was he in position? She couldn't comm him without her voice giving them away. The Marines' military comm implant suddenly made a whole lot of sense.

She caught sight of movement in the undergrowth where she'd sent Arthur.

Here goes nothing.

She rose to her feet, took her beamer from its holster, and stepped into the open. She could see over the bike now, and she found herself staring into the startled eyes of an Aboriginal man.

She said, "I don't want to—"

He leapt from his sleeping bag. He had a gun and was pointing it at her.

"I didn't mean to scare you," she said, wondering where Arthur had got to.

"I'm not scared," the man replied. "That was you tried to make me crash last night, right? Get out of here."

"I'm looking for—"

"You've got five seconds to leave."

"Let me explain."

"Four. Three."

Arthur's broad, tall frame broke through the vegetation on the other side of the small clearing. The man swiveled toward the king.

It was the distraction she needed. She raced out. As the man began to swing back to her, she threw herself on him and grappled him around the waist. They hit the dirt together. Her opponent was lithe and strong, but she soon had him on his front, his arm behind his back.

Arthur stood over them, nodding approvingly. "Now you can tell us where the children are."

13

He wasn't a man, he was a kid, Taylan realized as she turned him over. When he'd been pointing a gun at her he'd looked older, but now she could see he was only in his mid-to-late teens.

Arthur picked up the boy's weapon while he kept his own trained on him.

"If you promise not to try to escape," she said, "I won't tie you up. We just want to ask you some questions."

"I promise," the boy said quickly.

She released her hold on him.

Instantly, he leapt up. He ran five paces before she had him on his front in the dirt again.

"That was stupid," she said. "Arthur could have shot you."

In truth, he wouldn't have fired with her so near the boy, and if he had he would probably have missed.

"I *really* don't want to hurt you," she went on.

"Then get your knee off my back," the boy retorted, his grimacing face turned to one side.

"I only want to talk to you about some missing children."

The boy remained silent at first, then he said, "So what's with the surprise dawn attack? And the guns?"

Fair questions. "We couldn't take the risk you would leave on your motorbike. What's your name?"

"None of your business."

"Well, I'm Taylan and this is Arthur."

The boy spat dirt and answered, "Pleased to make your acquaintances. Now can you get off me? I won't run this time."

She let go of his wrist and stood up.

The boy turned over and, wiping soil from the side of his face, moved to a sitting position. "Can I get a drink?"

"Sure."

He stepped to his motorbike and filled a small cup of water from a canister on the side. After taking a sip, he swilled the water around his mouth and spat into the bushes. Then he drank the remainder. All the while, Arthur kept his gun trained on him.

Throwing him a surly look, the boy said, "Would you please put that thing away?"

Taylan motioned to Arthur and he complied, sliding his weapon back into his holster, though he continued to hold onto the boy's gun.

"Are you short on supplies?" she asked. "We have plenty. We could give you some in exchange for information."

"What information?"

"Have you seen or heard of any Crusader camps with children who look like they don't belong to them?"

"Crusaders, here in Oz? Let me think. Sit down. You're making me nervous."

They sat on the dry dirt away from the pool's edge. She crossed her legs and Arthur squatted on his haunches.

The kid stowed his cup and turned to one of the devices that had worried the king. He picked up the black box in one hand

and lifted the flap of one of his bike's panniers with the other, about to stash the device inside it. The device caught on the flap and overturned. Transparent tubes full of dirt spilled out.

The boy cursed and placed the equipment on the ground before gathering the dirt-filled tubes. They were stoppered so none had lost their contents. He began to replace them in their slots.

"What *is* that?" asked Taylan.

The box that had held the tubes couldn't be for storage. The slots only comprised a fifth of the structure. On the top was an interface screen with dials running down one edge.

"Never mind," the boy muttered.

"What are you doing out here?" she persisted. "We followed your trail all day yesterday. You've been zigzagging across the desert like a drunken spider. So you were digging in the dirt to take soil samples?"

"Damn, you guys ask a lot of questions! Why do you care what I'm doing?"

"I'm just curious. You led us quite a chase. Does that box analyze the samples?"

He scowled at her.

She held up her hands. "Sorry."

He settled down on top of his sleeping bag. "What makes you think there are Crusaders around here?"

"Not here exactly," replied Taylan. "North-west, nearer the arable land."

"There's not much in the way of farming country up there anymore. What was it you said about missing kids?"

"We have it on good authority that Crusaders have been trafficking children into the country, probably ahead of a planned invasion. But no one knows where they've been keeping them except it's likely to be somewhere remote in the north."

"Everywhere in the north is remote. You think *your* kids are with them, right?"

His frank gaze pierced her.

She looked down. "It's obvious, is it? Yes, I think—I hope—my kids are with them."

When she looked up, his expression wasn't as harsh. "We were expecting a Crusader invasion after the BI fell. Word is that won't be happening now."

"I really doubt it."

"You're from the BI, aren't you. I can tell by your accent. But you..." he turned to Arthur "...I can't tell where you're from."

"I'm from a long time ago," said the king.

The boy looked confused. They were getting off track. She felt he was deliberately avoiding answering her questions, but maybe he was only delaying to give himself time to think.

She decided to give him a little push. "Are you testing for minerals?"

"Huh? No!" He might as well have answered *Yes, absolutely.*

"Let me guess," she continued. "You're working for one of Ua Talman's mining companies."

It *was* a guess, but an educated one. It explained everything: the soil samples, the boy's cagey attitude, and the fact that he hadn't stopped last night after nearly running into their vehicle. Australia wasn't a dangerous place—aside from the wildlife. Meeting strangers in the outback shouldn't have been scary. But most types of mining were banned.

"No way," the boy protested. "I would never do anything illegal."

He gave a look of righteous outrage so exaggerated and utterly unconvincing Taylan and Arthur burst out laughing.

When she had recovered, she wiped her eyes and said, "We don't care what you're doing, but you should know all those unlicensed mining operations are being closed down. Talman's winding them up. He's mining asteroids from now on."

"What? *Shit!*"

"I thought you said you weren't involved with him?" Arthur asked dryly.

"I'm not! Only...shit." The boy got up and stomped over to his motorbike. He proceeded to remove the soil sample analyzer from the pannier, take out the tubes, pull out each stopper, and dump the contents on the ground.

Taylan and Arthur chuckled, though she felt sorry for him. The boy had lost his source of income, and money had to be hard to come by in this part of the world.

After he'd vented his disappointment and frustration, and ten or eleven small piles of dirt stood at his feet, the boy returned to his sleeping bag and sank onto it disconsolately.

"Crusaders, eh?" he asked, resting his elbow on his knee and his chin on his upturned palm.

"Yes," she replied. "Have you heard anything? Anything at all?"

"Well, I don't know if they were EAC, but there was a rumor about a group setting up in an area like the one you described. No one knew who they were except they were outsiders who didn't want anything to do with the locals. They were pretty hostile, in fact, from what I heard. No one mentioned any kids, but they might be the ones you're looking for."

"They could be," she said. "Do you know where they are?"

"No, it was just a bit of gossip, but I could try to find out for you."

"It would be great if you could. Do you have comm? We have it in our vehicle."

"I have it. It might take me a few hours to track down the information, though."

It wasn't a strong lead but it was worth pursuing. If the rumor was about the Crusader settlement, it could shorten the search by days or weeks.

"We can wait."

The boy returned to his bike and took out a hand-held comm.

As he spoke into it, Arthur got up. "I'll get some food for him to show our gratitude."

"Good idea," she replied. "I'll wait here." She didn't mention she was staying in case the kid changed his mind, as he could overhear her. Neither did she mention the other reason Arthur wanted to go back to their vehicle—to check on Excalibur.

After a short conversation, the boy put the comm away. "My auntie's going to ask around."

He sat down again and held out his hand. "I'm Kevin."

They shook.

"Sorry about your kids," he said.

"Thanks. Sorry about kneeling on your back."

He shrugged. "I can see why you're so desperate. My mum would tear down a brick wall with her bare hands to get to me if she had to. It's bad enough persuading her to let me come out here and take mineral samples. ...*Ooops*." He covered his mouth and grinned.

"What will you do now you're out of a job, Kevin?"

He shrugged again. "Buggered if I know. There's not a lot of work around here, and I can't move away. My mum would hate it. Not that I want to. I love it here. *Damn.* I really liked that work."

Arthur returned with the packets of food. As he handed them over, Taylan saw he'd picked out the meals they'd tried and hated. The king wasn't being generous so much as getting rid of unwanted supplies. Still, maybe Kevin would like them.

He thanked Arthur and turned over the rations, reading the labels.

"Hey," she said, "I have an idea. Why don't you come along with us? Arthur can pay you. He's loaded. Whether or not your auntie finds out where the Crusader settlement is, your knowledge of the local landscape could help us locate it."

Kevin looked up, surprised. "Sure, I can do that."

Later that day, when she was driving and Kevin was riding alongside their vehicle on his motorbike, she caught Arthur's expression of smug self-satisfaction.

"Just because we found Kevin," she said, "it doesn't mean you were right about Merlin's 'patterns'. Me being reunited with my kids won't make any difference to anyone except me and them."

Yet his smug expression didn't fade.

He couldn't have said *I told you so* any clearer if he'd tried.

14

They'd hit rough country. Up until this point in their journey, the ground had been relatively flat. The scrub clinging to life in the godforsaken place had been somewhat of an obstacle, but the spiny bushes were nothing compared to what they now faced. The ground rose and fell sharply, and though their vehicle and Kevin's motorbike were handling the inclines, they were traveling significantly slower. Fissures and gullies cut across their path too, forcing them to go kilometers out of their way.

The only saving grace was that Taylan had managed to comm the Search-and-Rescue coordinator, a man called Enzo Ricci, with the information Kevin's auntie had given them about the site of the rumored outsiders' camp. Ricci had been very interested in the news, saying it was an area they hadn't searched yet.

The way things were going it was likely the local team would find the Crusaders' camp before she did—if it was the Crusaders' camp. But it didn't matter who found her kids as long as they were finally safe.

The sun was heading for the horizon and they were still hours away from their destination. Her shoulder and arm muscles were sore from guiding the vehicle over the uneven landscape, and an old-fashioned smithy seemed to have set up shop behind her eyes, the hammering echoing through her head.

"We should stop here for the night," said Arthur, surveying the slightly flatter piece of ground they were currently traversing.

"No, we can still make another few kilometers before we lose the light entirely."

Even *she* had to admit she was in no shape to be driving using night vision in that unpredictable terrain.

"If we don't stop here," Arthur countered, "we might be forced to camp on a hill."

Kevin waved at them from his bike.

She braked and lowered her window. The desert heat wafted in.

The kid drew up beside her and removed his helmet. "We should camp here. It's not going to get any flatter ahead."

Damn. It was two against one and she was too tired to argue. She sighed. "All right."

"Can I hook my bike up to your battery? It's either that or wait while it charges up in the morning."

"Honestly, I don't know if that's gonna work, but if you can figure it out, yeah, no problem."

She asked Arthur to set up their sleeping arrangement while she tried to help Kevin.

A quarter of an hour later, the tent that extended from the back of their vehicle was up. They had about another half an hour of daylight, but the moon had risen already and it was full. The lunar beams coupled with the starlight would mean a bright night in the outback, but it would be cold too.

"Do you want to sleep in our tent tonight?" she asked Kevin after they finally correctly attached the wires. "It'll be a squeeze. Arthur seems even bigger lying down. But you're welcome."

"Nah, I prefer sleeping out in the open. That's another reason I liked that soil sampling job. It gave me an excuse to tramp around the desert without Mum giving me an earful."

"Sorry that's over for you. Maybe you can find something else to do."

"Yeah, maybe," he replied, though he didn't sound hopeful.

Arthur emerged from the tent. "I set everything up and emptied the condenser." He eyed the motorbike. "What are you doing with that?"

"Just making sure Kevin can ride all day tomorrow without running out of power."

"Ah, I see."

Taylan doubted he did. As far as she could tell, he didn't really grasp the concept of electricity.

Something appeared to be bothering him.

"What's wrong?"

"Nothing. Only... We have a little daylight left. I was wondering if I could ride the machine."

Kevin's eyebrows rose. "Ride my motorbike?"

"Umm..." Taylan was equally bemused.

"It's been a long while since I rode a horse," Arthur explained. "I was wondering if it was the same."

"I'm pretty sure it isn't," said Kevin, sharing a look with Taylan, "but if that's what you want, be my guest. Just be careful not to crash. The nearest garage is about two hundred K from here."

She said softly, "I'm not sure this is such a good idea."

But Arthur was already climbing on the bike, his hands on the handlebars.

"Better put on my helmet," said Kevin, handing it over. "Sorry, it's a bit sweaty. It's been a long day's ride."

It was soon clear the helmet was too small for Arthur's big head and bushy hair. He would have to go without, which made Taylan even less certain this was a good idea.

Kevin explained how to accelerate, brake, and change gears. He didn't say anything about turning the bike but she guessed the principle was the same as turning a horse's head. Arthur would figure that out by himself. The king was nodding as if he understood, but how could he? Even she would struggle with changing gears. Every vehicle she'd ever been in had changed gears automatically. The bike was from another time altogether, but then again so was Arthur.

Kevin finished giving his instructions and stepped back.

"Take it slow, Arthur," she advised.

Not only were they days from a garage, they were also days from the nearest hospital. What would the BA say if their precious king got hurt while in her company?

"Don't worry," he replied. "I won't be trying any fast gallops."

Kevin shared another look with Taylan.

Arthur retracted the kickstand and started up the bike.

She put her hands to her cheeks, anticipating a disaster.

The king put the bike in gear and gently twisted the throttle while also lifting his feet onto the pegs. The motorbike lurched forward.

She covered her eyes and peeked between her fingers.

He wobbled forward a few meters but then had to turn to avoid a bush. The bike swerved hard and overbalanced, though Arthur managed to stay upright. He straightened up the bike and tried again.

"You know," Kevin remarked as the king rode slowly on. "He's not doing too badly for a first try."

She couldn't help agreeing.

The kid didn't know who Arthur was. She hadn't mentioned anything about him and Kevin hadn't asked. He clearly assumed the king was just a friend helping her to find her children. He didn't realize exactly how remarkable it was that a man from the Dark Ages was taking to motorbike riding with ease.

She removed her hands from her face. Arthur was wobbling around their campsite slowly, but he hadn't been forced to stop again. As she watched, he became a little more confident, speeding up and expanding the area he covered. Soon, he was zooming along, the wind in his hair.

Smiling, she watched him.

The setting sun and encroaching darkness seemed to signal to Arthur it was time to stop. He rode the bike back.

He wore a goofy grin as he braked and turned off the engine. She remembered the sad, depressed man who had come to see her in prison. What a transformation he'd undergone. She was glad she'd agreed to him joining her in her search, and that Hans Jonte had fixed things so he didn't cause a diplomatic incident.

"You did great," said Kevin.

"Thank you. It was very enjoyable. I'd like to ride your machine again another time."

"Maybe when we get where we're going. Riding over the kind of ground we covered today is a bit different from riding on the flat."

"I'll hook it up to our cell again," said Taylan.

When she was finished, they each got themselves something to eat and sat on a blanket Arthur had retrieved from their vehicle. She pulled the tab on her ration packet and waited for the contents to heat up.

The red desert had turned monochrome and the stars were coming out, thick and bright. The pale disc of the moon hung over their heads, and the air was turning cool and fresh. She could see why Kevin preferred sleeping outside at night.

The boy dug into the contents of his meal pack with a spoon. He was eating one of the meals Arthur had given him this morning. As he put the full spoon in his mouth, his nose instantly wrinkled.

"You guys gave me the shit food, right?"

15

––––––––

They had driven all morning and then stopped briefly for lunch when the news came. Arthur was having another go on Kevin's motorbike while Kevin sat in the passenger seat eating a sandwich. The windows were down and Taylan had noticed a change in the air. For most of their journey it had been arid, sucking the sweat from her skin. Now, it held a tinge of moisture. They were near the borderlands where crops could be teased from the soil.

The comm console bleeped twice. Someone was trying to get in contact.

Her heart lifted when she saw the name of the caller.

"Any news?" she asked Enzo Ricci as soon as his face appeared on the screen.

"Good-ish news. We found a camp—"

"Great!"

"But it's been abandoned. Whoever made it is long gone. From what we can tell it was pretty big, at least a hundred or so people lived here, but it looks like they upped sticks several days ago. I'm sorry. I know it isn't exactly what you want to hear, but we're working on it."

Her heart sank. "It's okay. It's something."

"I'll send the coordinates. They left a trail and it isn't hard to follow. Some helis are tracking it now and we'll see what we see."

"What kind of trail?"

"Horses and wagons."

"So it has to be Crusaders?"

"I'd bet good money on it."

"If it *is* the child traffickers, they must have taken the children with them. They marched them in from the coast so they would march them across country too."

"I would think so," said Ricci. "What are your children's names?"

"Patrin and Kayla. Patrin's eight and Kayla's three, nearly four, but she's tall for her age."

Two of Patrin's and one of Kayla's birthdays had passed while she'd been separated from them.

Ricci said, "I'll comm you the minute I know anything."

"Thanks."

"I'm just doing my job. The thanks should go to whoever tipped us off with the location. We didn't think the Crusaders would be living so far inland."

"That would be Kevin," said Taylan.

The boy leaned over into view of the comm and waved.

"Thanks, mate," said Ricci. "Couldn't have done it without you."

The screen went blank.

So Arthur had been right It was only because they'd spoken to Kevin that the Crusaders' camp had been found so quickly.

Could there really be a 'pattern' shaping the events of people's lives? She still couldn't see why her reuniting with her children should make any difference in the grand scheme of things. There were plenty of parents who would never see their kids again. Why should her family be any different?

She reminded herself to not get her hopes up too much. Ricci had only found the remains of a camp. She was a long way from holding Patrin and Kayla in her arms again.

She honked the horn to get Arthur's attention. They had to leave immediately.

IT WAS after dark before they neared the coordinates Ricci had sent. Taylan had driven on after sunset, using night vision to navigate the rough ground and leaving Kevin behind, his bike's battery dead. He would join them later when his battery had recharged.

One eye on the map on the dashboard and one on the terrain, she wondered why they hadn't caught sight of the abandoned camp yet. According to the map, it was only a kilometer away. Then their vehicle crested a rise and light washed over the windscreen. She braked and turned off the night vision.

Brilliant floodlights illuminated a patch of ground directly ahead. A circular area of worn, bare earth stood out from the rest and two trails led away from it, one thickly rutted with wheel tracks and pocked with horses' hooves—the trail Ricci's helis were following.

She hadn't heard anything from him since his earlier comm. That had to mean either the helis hadn't caught up to the Crusader wagons or they had but no children had been discovered.

Search-and-Rescue vehicles dotted the place, and four large tents had been set up outside the former encampment. There were also several substantial ash piles where, she presumed, the Crusaders had torched wooden dwellings or other structures.

Arthur laid a hand on her forearm. "Don't worry. I am sure your children will be found."

"Well," she replied tremulously, "there's no guarantee they were here, but I feel closer to them now than ever."

"That's a good sign."

She drove down the incline.

Someone must have noticed their vehicle approaching because Ricci appeared from a tent and walked out to meet them. He looked tired and worried, and as he shook Arthur and Taylan's hands.

He said to the king, "Pleased to meet you, Your..."

"Just call me Arthur."

She thought she saw something more than general stress and fatigue behind Ricci's eyes.

"Can I talk to you in private?" he asked Taylan after the formalities were out of the way.

It was as if time stopped.

"W-what?" she asked, though she'd heard him perfectly well.

"I'll take a look around," Arthur said, He patted Taylan's shoulder before leaving.

Ricci's serious expression grew more solemn. "We found some children. Not long after I comm'd you, a couple of kids walked in from the bush. They must have seen us arrive and figured out we were the good guys. They were in a bad way. We started treatment and they're doing all right. We'll fly them to Cairns in the morning."

She filled in the information he'd left out. "They're not my kids."

He shook his head. "They're twin girls, about five years old. We couldn't get a lot out of them, but they seemed to think the Crusaders didn't take the smaller children with them."

"Okay."

She didn't know what to make of what he was saying. The

Crusaders had brought children here, and that meant they could have brought *her* kids here. But if the little girls had been alone when the rescuers arrived, they must have been abandoned. They'd been living here without food or water, possibly for days.

Ricci sighed heavily. "After those two turned up, we searched the surrounding area thoroughly and we found three more kids. They aren't doing so well. We haven't been able to find out their names or anything."

"Can I see them?"

"Yeah, of course. I just wanted you to be prepared."

She guessed what he was trying to tell her was the children she was about to see—possibly Patrin and Kayla—might not survive. That she might be seeing them only in order to say goodbye.

"I want to see them," she said doggedly.

He led her to the large tent he'd emerged from when she and Arthur had arrived. He lifted the flap and she stepped in. What she saw halted her in her tracks. Six low cots stood along the edges, five of them holding a sunburned, emaciated child. They were hooked up to drips and sleeping, most likely sedated.

"It's safer to stabilize them here before trying to move them to a hospital," Ricci explained.

"These are the girls?" she whispered, pointing at the two nearest cots.

The similarity between the blonde-haired children lying in them was plain to see, despite their red, burned skin.

"That's them. They aren't too badly off. It's the other three the doctor is worried about."

Taylan was already moving toward the opposite side of the tent. She bent down to study the faces of the sleeping children closely.

How many times had she done this exact thing? When

she'd been searching for Patrin and Kayla in the refugee camps in Ireland, she must have looked at the faces of thousands of children. And in the streets of Irish towns and West BI, she must have looked at tens of thousands more, her heart missing a beat whenever she saw a boy with eyes like Patrin's or the back of a girl's head that resembled Kayla's. Each time she'd come down to Earth with a thump when she realized it wasn't them.

These poor children in the tent had been through a terrible ordeal, it was plain to see. Their thin, starved bodies seemed to be clinging to life by a thread. She hoped with all her might they would live, but...

She straightened up and faced Ricci. Forcing the words from her constricted throat, she said, "None of them are mine."

At her announcement, his face fell further and he turned pale. "Let's go outside."

He set off walking, forcing her to follow. He didn't speak. She kept up with him all the way to the edge of the Crusader camp, where he stopped.

Close-up, the paths between the places where the dwellings had been were plain to see, smooth lines in the soil. How long had the camp been here? When had her children come here? West BI had fallen to the EAC last of all the Isles, and then it would have taken time for the Crusaders to bring the kids halfway around the globe. She guessed this might have been Patrin and Kayla's home for eighteen months or longer.

Or maybe they'd never been here. Maybe they were in another Crusader encampment. Maybe they'd never come to Australia.

Ricci drew in a deep breath and exhaled slowly.

"You see that?" he nodded at a pile of ashes near the center of the camp. No smoke drifted up from it. The wind stirred the cold cinders. It must have burnt out days ago.

She replied softly, "Uh huh."

"We checked through it, looking for...well, any clue we might find about what went on here. We found..." He swallowed.

She turned from the ashy heap. "No."

"We don't know if they were locked in..."

She began walking away from him.

"...or if they were hiding there when the place was set alight," he said to her retreating back. "I'm sorry. I had to tell you, but it might not be..."

His voice faded from her hearing. A rushing sound was in her ears and she couldn't see where she was going. She marched on regardless, until she walked directly into someone tall and broad.

"Taylan," Arthur said, catching her shoulders, "did you find your—"

"Fuck you!" She slammed her fists into him. "Fuck you and your fucking pattern!"

She collapsed, sobbing, onto the dirt.

16

It was the early hours of the morning and Taylan had cried herself dry. For months she'd held things together the best she could, forcing herself to not let go of hope like she had when she'd enlisted in the Marines. She'd bottled everything up for so long. But the news about the dead children, coming after days of exhausting travel and fragile dreams of success, had broken her. Now she felt nothing. She was hollow and empty inside.

She sat up. She was alone. She vaguely remembered Arthur bringing her here to their tent and trying to comfort her. He must have given up and gone off to a quieter spot to sleep.

She got to her feet. She'd been on top of her sleeping bag fully clothed. The night's chill had infiltrated the tent and penetrated to her bones. She wasn't hungry or thirsty despite not eating or drinking for hours.

She went out. All was quiet. The rescue team was sleeping, their vehicles and tents dark. Lights shining on the abandoned camp had been dimmed, lending the place a ghostly air.

She remembered the children who had died, and she shuddered.

At the edges of the site the beams of light faded away and darkness encroached. She tried to remember where the track made by the Crusader wagons lay. Orienting herself, she walked toward it, skirting the piles of ash.

The ruts were wide and deep in the soft earth. The traffickers had left by a different route from the one they usually took, where the ground had been compacted. They'd gone farther inland, toward the desert. What they imagined they would find there, she couldn't tell. She'd come that way herself and there was nothing there but a slow death once their supplies ran out. Unless they were heading for a rendezvous with another group, or perhaps they had a plan for escaping the country.

She followed the trail, walking in the ruts.

Angular shapes seemed to loom up on her left, startling her. Three helis sat on a flat, empty area of ground. They'd returned from their mission to follow the Crusaders' trail. Had they found the wagons? The cockpits were empty.

She walked on.

All remnants of artificial light gone, only moonlight and starlight shining out briefly from between scudding clouds guided her. Yet the trail was easy to navigate, its lines deeper shades than the surrounding shadow. Had Patrin and Kayla come this way? It seemed unlikely. If they'd managed to escape as the Crusaders left, why would they have followed their captors? It would have made more sense to take their chances in the surrounding scrub like the other children had. But Ricci's searchers hadn't found any more kids.

Her mind turning numb, she walked. Slowly, the clouds dispersed and the moonlight shone down strongly, turning the red earth silvery white. The noises of nocturnal animals broke the night quiet: cries, calls, and the rustle of bodies moving through the bush.

Hours passed.

She became aware her leg muscles were aching. Thirstiness had gradually wormed its way into her consciousness. She halted, becoming more aware of her surroundings. Turning, she looked back. How far had she come? The sky in the east was lightening and a rosy tinge softened the horizon.

She had no water, no comm, and she hadn't told anyone where she was going. She didn't even have a hat. The sun would be up soon and its rays would be brutal.

She should go back.

But the thought of returning to the place where Patrin and Kayla might have lived made her want to vomit. Were her children's bodies among those found in the ashes? Had they died there, terrified out of their minds? If that was so, she didn't want to know. It was better to not know.

She wouldn't go back.

She couldn't.

She walked on.

The ruts the wagons had worn in the rusty earth sharpened in the brightening daylight. Between them were the regular pockmarks of iron-shod horses' hooves.

Patrin had always had a thing about horses. He'd loved them, and she'd been saving up to get him riding lessons.

I'm thinking about him in the past tense.

A painful lump formed in her throat and tears swelled in her dry, itchy eyes. If Patrin and Kayla were gone, there was no point in carrying on.

A sensation of warmth spread over her back. The sun was coming up.

Still, she walked.

Her thirstiness was unbearable. Though she continued to think about her kids, she began to scan the landscape almost unconsciously as her body sought water. Arthur's comment about signs of moist ground in terms of different, stronger growing, vegetation arose from her memory, but she saw nothing like that around her, only the spiny shrubs.

The nocturnal animals had returned to their daytime hide-outs. All was silent save for the quiet *hush* of the breeze.

The sun began to hammer on her back, neck, and the back of her head. The utter foolishness of what she was doing ran like a thread through her mind, but she was without hope. It was better to keep walking.

Heat rose, reflected from the ground, shimmering air.

Her legs were aching terribly now. Her tongue was thick in her mouth and a painful band had tightened around her head. Breathing in the dusty atmosphere took effort. The act of putting one foot in front of the other had become arduous labor. Her toes frequently caught on the uneven ground.

She fell heavily, the red earth seeming to rise up to meet her. Suddenly, she was flat on her face on the dusty ground. She turned onto her back. The sun was directly overhead, a white-gold orb floating in a pale blue sea, unbearably bright.

She lay still, burning in the glow, for an unknown length of time. She opened her eyes, not remembering closing them. The sun had changed position and moved to the other half of the sky.

Unwilling to stay still any longer, she turned onto her hands and knees and forced herself to her feet. She tottered on.

The sun faced her now as if trying to bar her way. Her exposed skin burned while the skin beneath her clothes merely cooked in the heat. Soon, she didn't need to squint. Her swelling eyelids did the work on their own.

When the sun began to set her strength finally gave out.

One minute she was stumbling along the track, remotely aware the brightness ahead of her was fading and her raw skin was cooling, and the next minute she was horizontal. A baked rut jutted into her chest but she didn't have the energy to move off it. The soil radiated its heat into her bare skin.

She was dipping out, losing consciousness, but there wasn't anything she could do about it. There wasn't anything she *wanted* to do about it. The welcome oblivion began to overwhelm her.

Just as she was going under, voices impinged on the edge of her awareness.

Patrin and Kayla were arguing.

"I *told* you it was her," said Kayla petulantly. "I told you it was Mammy."

"I was only saying it wasn't safe to come out until we were sure," Patrin replied.

"But I *was* sure, and now she's gone to sleep."

Patrin and Kayla.

Ever since she'd given them to the older woman so she could defend the villagers, they'd rarely left her mind. How typical it was they should invade her thoughts at a time like this, when she was nearly at the end. She wished so much she'd been able to find them. Giving them into another's care was the greatest regret of her life, though it had seemed the right thing to do at the time. How often had she cursed and berated herself for her stupidity? Or tortured herself imagining the suffering they'd undergone due to her thoughtlessness?

"Mammy, wake up," Patrin said.

"Please wake up," Kayla echoed.

The dream continued, holding back the encroaching darkness.

It even became tactile as she felt small hands on her shoulders.

"Don't sleep," Kayla continued. "We want to go home now."

"I can't take you home," Taylan mumbled. "It's too far." She recalled the fresh green hills of her homeland, the cool, moist air, the seemingly endless rain. She remembered walking in the forest with Meilyr and his brothers on their way to Ynys Môn, and the mountain where Wright had found Arthur. It all seemed so long ago.

Kayla was weeping.

"Shhh," Taylan soothed. "Don't cry."

"*I want to go home!*"

She sounded so real.

Perhaps because she'd recovered for a few minutes from her hours of walking, or perhaps it was her child's crying calling to something deep inside her, but a shock hit Taylan's core.

Kayla *was* real.

She was really here.

Taylan's eyes snapped open.

Patrin and Kayla were looking down at her. They were nut brown, sunburned in places, and their hair had become burnished bronze. They were older and thinner than she remembered them too. But they were undeniably her children.

She jerked upright, gasping as she grabbed them into her arms.

Speechless with joy, she held onto them tightly, reveling in the feel of their small bodies against hers.

"You woke up!" said Kayla.

"I knew you would come," Patrin whispered as he clung to her. "I knew you would find us."

"I missed you, Mammy," Kayla said. "I missed you so much."

"I missed you too," Taylan croaked. "I'm so sorry I didn't stay with you and keep you safe."

"It's all right," Patrin replied. "You had to fight the soldiers."

"And you found us now," said Kayla.

Taylan hugged her children tightly, vowing to never let them out of her sight again.

But then the reality of their situation began to filter in.

"Do you have any water?" asked Patrin.

"No, I haven't." She relaxed her hold sufficiently to look into her kids' faces. "What are you doing out here?"

"We followed the wagons," said Patrin. "I knew there was no water near the camp, so after we ran away, I thought we should go with the Crusaders anyway, only at a distance. That way we might be able to get food and water. There was a girl with them who helped us. Her name is Hannah, but that isn't her real name. I don't know what her real name is." He looked down. "Two days ago they caught her sneaking out to us. They beat her. I could hear them. Kayla and I hid so they wouldn't find us. We stopped following the wagons after that."

"It's been two days since you had anything to drink?"

"We had some water left over, but we drank the last of it yesterday."

"I'm thirsty," said Kayla. "Can you get me some water, Mammy?"

Taylan didn't reply. Not only didn't she have any water, they were tens of kilometers from help and she hadn't brought along any comm. If she tried to take them back to the camp, *she* wouldn't make it, let alone her kids.

After her long search and her children's survival in perilous circumstances, her family was finally reunited—only to face death in the wilderness.

17

"It's getting cold," said Patrin. "We need to go to our den."

"Your den?" Taylan asked.

"It's this way." He tugged on her hand. "You're sick, aren't you, Mam?"

"I am, but seeing you two has made me feel a whole lot better."

She struggled to her feet. Whatever chemicals her brain had released at the surprise encounter with her children had washed away her exhaustion and debilitation, but the effect would only be temporary. She needed to do everything possible she could to prolong their lives until help arrived. But what could she realistically do?

Patrin continued to hold her hand and Kayla took the other as her son led her from the rutted track into the bush. About twenty meters from the trail stood a shrub larger than the others and on the other side of it was a shallow hole large enough for two children. Lying in the hole was a piece of hessian—a sack that had been opened out to make a blanket.

This was Patrin's 'den' he'd clearly made to try to keep himself and his sister warm overnight.

The pain of seeing the evidence of her children's suffering was almost too much for Taylan. She bit her lip hard.

"This is where you sleep?" she asked.

Patrin nodded.

"You did a great job, sweetheart."

"But you're too big to fit," said Kayla. "We have to dig a bigger hole."

"But the sack's still too small for all of us," said Patrin, his voice wobbling.

"Don't worry," Taylan said. "We'll figure it out."

Kayla asked, "Can't we go to your friends? Your friends will have water."

"My friends are very far away."

"Oh."

"But they'll be looking for me, and when they find me they'll find you too."

She believed this was probably true. She wasn't sure how long it would have taken for Arthur or Ricci to realize she was missing, but a day had passed since she'd walked out of the camp. They had to know by now she wasn't coming back. She hated that she'd made more work for the team when they already had plenty to do. On the other hand, if she hadn't taken her suicidal walk into the bush, she might never have found her kids. Without water, they wouldn't have lasted more than two days at most, and Ricci hadn't mentioned anything about searching for children along the trail.

Would he find them in time? He had no idea where she was and they were all severely dehydrated already. He could send up his helis and drones to scan for heat signatures, but they had hundreds of square kilometers to cover. And once the sun was up, the pilots and drones would be working on visual only.

Had the Crusaders' wagons been found? Presumably, as the helis had been following their trail and the wagons had to be moving slowly. How that might factor into her and her children's rescue, though, she had no idea. Perhaps it would be best to return to the track in the morning. That might increase their chances of being spotted.

None of them could go any further. It was best to stay here, close to the trail.

Then it would be a matter of waiting and hoping help arrived in time.

Patrin was scooping the dirt at one edge of the depression with his bare hands to enlarge it.

"Don't do that," Taylan said. "I'll do it. You sit down with your sister."

As she bent to the ground, Patrin put an arm around Kayla and settled next to her.

"You did really well looking after Kayla."

"I had to carry her a bit, but she isn't very heavy."

Taylan wondered if her son had carried his sister on the long walk from the coast. It must have been so hard for them both, but especially Patrin. He would have a better under-standing of the danger they were in and he would have felt responsible for Kayla too.

The dry soil crumbled beneath her fingers as she dug into it. In a few minutes, she'd created space for herself. She picked up the square of hessian and told her children to come and lie down. Then she curled up next to them and covered them in the makeshift blanket. Holding them close, she was dismayed to feel how thin and bony they'd become.

"Why did it take you so long to find us?" Kayla complained.

"I tried," Taylan whispered. "I looked hard for a long time."

"Be quiet, Kayla," said Patrin. "Mam found us in the end and that's all that matters."

"I'm thirsty," Kayla grumbled.

"Try to go to sleep," said Taylan. "Maybe help will come in the morning." She wanted them to conserve what little energy they had left.

The air had turned chilly, but she had the body heat of her kids to keep her warm. More importantly, they were all together again.

Despite their feeble state or perhaps because of it, the two children quickly fell asleep. When they were breathing deeply and regularly, Taylan felt herself grow sleepy too. The battle between joy and despair going on within her eased and she closed her eyes.

Seemingly only a short while later, the sound of crying woke her.

It was Kayla. She was sitting cross-legged in the darkness, pale in the moonlight, her filthy, worn dress tight over her knees, hunched over, rocking and wailing.

"I'm *thirsty*! I'm *thirsty*! I want a *drink*!"

"We don't have any water," Patrin scolded from his prone position. "Lie down and go to sleep."

"Come here," Taylan said, sitting up and holding out her arms.

Kayla climbed over her brother, extracting a groan of annoyance. Holding onto her, Taylan stood up and carried her away so Patrin might go back to sleep. Her child's sweet head buried under her chin as she walked, she didn't think she'd ever felt so wretched.

What time was it? How long had they slept? She couldn't tell from the moon's position, not knowing when it had risen.

Kayla's crying hadn't lessened. If anything it had grown louder, though few tears escaped her eyes. She also felt too hot. As the youngest of them, she would be the most vulnerable to dehydration.

If only they had water, just a little, enough to keep them going until they were found. Not even water in particular. Any liquid would do as long as it didn't make them sick. The sap from a plant might work but all the bushes were dry and spiny. Or an animal's blood. If she could catch and kill something they could drink its blood. But the desert animals were too wary to put themselves at risk. She'd heard plenty of them but she'd never spotted one.

What was she thinking? She didn't need to catch anything.

Setting Kayla down, she scanned her immediate surroundings. The moonlight was casting long, deep shadows and highlighting the vegetation and rocks. She picked up a stone, but it was soft-edged and too blunt. Picking up another, she ran her fingers over it. This one was better but still not sufficiently sharp. The third one held a narrower edge. She pressed it against her wrist and sawed at her flesh.

It only grazed her skin and didn't cut it.

Kayla had stopped crying. "What are you doing?"

"I'm trying to find a sharp stone. Can you help me?"

Her daughter didn't move. "Why do you want a sharp stone?"

Taylan squatted down and put one stone on the ground before smashing another into it. When nothing resulted, she tried again. On her fourth try, a small flake broke off the lower stone. She picked it up and pushed it into her wrist. It sliced into her skin and she sucked air between her teeth at the painful stinging sensation.

"What are you doing, Mammy?" Kayla repeated, quieter.

Drops of blood welled up and began to flow.

Taylan dug deeper, her jaw clenching.

"Here," she gasped, holding out her wrist, "drink this."

But Kayla backed away, horror in her eyes.

"It's okay," Taylan tried to reassure her. "It'll help you feel better."

"No, Mammy! No!" She began to wail again.

Then, over the sound of her child's cries, Taylan heard another sound.

An engine.

An engine!

Was it a heli?

She rose to her feet and searched the skies but she couldn't see a black form blocking out the starlight. How to attract the searcher's attention? If only she could make a fire.

Blood dripped from her cut wrist onto the parched soil.

The engine noise was growing louder. She swiveled, trying to figure out its direction. They were so close to being saved if she could just attract the searcher's attention.

Grabbing Kayla into her arms, she ran to Patrin.

He'd heard the noise too and was sitting up, surprise and hope written over his features.

Then the engine cut out.

"No," Taylan muttered. "No, no, no!"

Where had the sound come from? Why had the engine stopped?

Anticipation they would be saved had sharpened her foggy mind, and she realized the noise couldn't have been a heli. She hadn't heard the whirr of rotor blades. It had to be a land vehicle, and that meant it was probably on the Crusaders' trail.

"Patrin, come with me."

Gripping his hand tightly and balancing her long-legged daughter on one hip, she hurried through the scrub.

Something was moving toward them.

Not something. Some*one*.

"Taylan?" a voice called.

Arthur.

"I'm here," she yelled back, her voice cracked, sobs of relief rising in her throat. "We're here!"

"I know," he replied. "You're still as noisy as a stallion after a mare in heat."

18

———

Arthur watched gravely as the medic bound Taylan's wrist. She was in the small hospital tent, sitting on the edge of a cot.

"How did you get this injury?" he asked.

Taylan looked down. "I don't remember."

Patrin and Kayla were sleeping, sedated while they received rehydration fluid. The doctor had said they were remarkably healthy considering their ordeal. They were sunburned and dehydrated but their vital organs were functioning well. It was only when she'd received the good news that Taylan had allowed anyone to treat her. The other children had gone from the tent, flown out of the camp the previous evening.

The madness of the last twenty-four hours was only just easing—the depths of her despair as she'd walked all day in the bush, the height of her joy when she'd found her kids, or rather, they'd found her, and the plummet into horror when she realized they might all die.

Had she really cut herself open to try to save Kayla's life? It had seemed reasonable in the circumstances.

"Arthur, I don't know how I can ever thank you for—"

"Shh. I won't hear your thanks. You prevented me from committing a great sin once. You may have saved my eternal soul from endless torment. Finding you in the wilderness is nothing compared to that."

What?

Just when he was beginning to seem like a normal person he came out with stuff like this. She guessed he was referring to the time she stopped him from killing Kala Orr.

"How did you know where I was?" she asked.

"I followed your trail. I am sorry to say it wasn't until darkness fell we realized you might be in danger. Until then, everyone assumed you were searching the immediate area for your children. Ricci sent up drones to look for your body's heat, and I looked for fresh footprints leading away from the camp. The light on the motorbike is very bright and allowed me to see them easily. Yours were the only fresh tracks that led far away and didn't turn back."

"Well, you might not count it as much of a favor, but I'm forever in your debt."

"It was no trouble. It brings me joy to see you reunited with your children."

She looked at Patrin and Kayla again. She actually found it hard to take her eyes off them, as if they might disappear without her constant vigilance.

"You're done," said the medic. "You should get some sleep."

While Taylan and Arthur had talked, she'd been applying ointment to Taylan's burned face. It was nearly dawn, and the sound of the camp waking up infiltrated the tent.

Taylan adjusted her position carefully to avoid snagging the line from her drip as she lay down and the medic left.

She told Arthur, "I don't want to go to sleep."

"You're worried that when you wake up your children might be gone?"

She nodded.

"I could ask the doctor for medicine to help you relax."

"No, I definitely don't want that. Could you stay and talk to me?"

He pulled up a chair.

"What's been happening while I was gone?"

"The Crusader wagons have been found, but they haven't been approached yet. Today, a combined operation will take place to secure the scene with minimal bloodshed. Ricci is preparing to receive the children and assess and treat them before they travel onward."

When she'd returned to the camp, she'd noticed more tents were being erected. So the place would be filled with kids? That would be nice but bittersweet, considering the ones who hadn't survived.

"From what the twin girls said," Arthur went on, "it seems the children were forced to take different names. But as the Crusaders only took the older children, this shouldn't be a problem when it comes to reuniting them with their families."

The kids' parents might have been killed during the invasion or afterward. There might not be anyone left to meet the children when they returned home.

"Do we know why they were driving their wagons into the desert?" she asked. "It would make more sense for them to head to the coast if they wanted to escape."

"Ricci guesses they may have been on their way to meet up with other Crusader groups, perhaps in order to disperse the children within Australian society and avoid discovery. As the EAC is collapsing, no ships will arrive to take the children out of the country. And where would they take them? It would be impossible to take them back to the BI now without their crime being discovered, and taking them to another Crusader territory would only be delaying the inevitable."

"I suppose we should be grateful they didn't just kill them all," she said bitterly.

"That would certainly be a hard thing to do, even for the most depraved Crusader, but perhaps they were also worried about leaving behind evidence of their crime."

She thought of the bodies in the ashes. "Too late for that."

"Indeed," said Arthur sadly.

The tent flap lifted and Kevin appeared, his face wreathed in smiles. "I just heard you were back! Congratulations on finding your kids."

"Thanks."

He peered at the two sleeping forms. "What a pair of cuties. You must be relieved."

"More than relieved. Words can't describe it. I'd been looking for them for so long, not really knowing if they were still alive. Thank you for lending Arthur your bike."

"No worries. It was the least I could do when I heard you were missing. Are they okay?"

"They'll be fine in a day or two the doctor said, though it might take them some time to get over the trauma of what happened to them."

"Yeah, of course," said Kevin. "Stands to reason. Still, they're back, right? That's the main thing."

"Yeah, absolutely."

The teenager stuck his hands in his pockets and said shyly, "I've got some good news of my own. Ricci offered me a job with Search-and-Rescue. Not volunteering, a proper full-time job. He said he needed someone with contacts in the region."

"That's fantastic news," said Taylan.

Arthur slapped his back, sending him stumbling forward.

"I'm stoked," he said. "Ricci reckons that now things are calming down a bit the tourists will start coming back. A few of them always wander off into the bush, not understanding what they're getting themselves into."

"You're the ideal man for the job," said Arthur.

"I don't know about that," Kevin replied. "Your tracking

skills put mine to shame. Seems to me *you'd* have a lot to offer Search-and-Rescue too."

"Ah, no. Now Taylan's children have been found, I must return to London. I have no excuse for staying away from my duties any longer."

"Fair enough. I thought you'd probably both be leaving soon. I'll be sad to see you go. We had some fun, didn't we?"

"We did," said Taylan. "But we can keep in touch. And maybe Arthur and I will be back one day."

"I hope so," said Kevin.

He still didn't know who Arthur was. He had no idea he'd spent the last couple of days in the company of the King of the Britannic Isles. Taylan didn't see any point in enlightening him.

"Or you could visit me in the Isles," Arthur said.

Kevin shivered. "No, thanks. I hate the cold."

Taylan laughed. "Very wise."

"I'll let you get some sleep," said Kevin. "Ricci's asked me to help set up tents for the kids. They should be here by this evening."

After he left, Taylan asked Arthur, "Do you have to go back to London soon? Can't you squeeze another few days' leave from your duties?"

"Unfortunately not. The BI Government has apparently been trumpeting my success in locating the missing children all over the media. I'm expected to return and attend interviews and social events."

"I'm sorry."

"It doesn't matter. This experience has been a welcome break. I feel better now and I have a better understanding of why I am here."

"Why you're here?"

"There was clearly some purpose to my helping you find your children."

Uh oh. He was going to talk about 'patterns' again.

"Arthur, I'm beyond grateful for your help and I can't express how happy and relieved I am to have Kayla and Patrin back again, but don't you think it could just be a coincidence?"

"No, I don't, though I don't see the end of the path we're on."

She was too tired to argue and she didn't care whether he was right. She didn't care about anything now her children were with her. She would never let them out of her sight again.

"I see the end of *my* path," she said. "A small house in a small town, a job that pays enough to survive, and a quiet, peaceful life bringing up my kids."

He shook his head.

"Huh?"

"I didn't want to tell you until after you'd recovered," he said, "but the Britannic Alliance is holding a meeting aboard the *Dauntless*, and your attendance is compulsory."

19

———

The surviving trafficked children were arriving. Taylan wanted to go out and help the rescuers but she couldn't bring herself to leave Patrin and Kayla. Instead, she stood at the entrance to the hospital tent and held it open when a child needing treatment was brought in. Fortunately, most of the kids seemed in reasonable shape. Only two had arrived so far and they'd walked in unassisted.

She glanced behind her at Patrin and Kayla. She found it hard to take her eyes off them, and whenever she looked at them joy leapt in her heart. Even Arthur's news about the meeting she was supposed to attend couldn't dampen her spirits.

What was *that* about, and why did she have to go?

Could the Alliance really make her?

She wasn't sure they could. She wasn't a Marine or a prisoner any longer. On the other hand, it seemed churlish to refuse. If it weren't for the Alliance's help in kitting her and Arthur out for the search, Patrin and Kayla might have died before she found them.

She shrugged and put the question aside. Now she had her kids back, nothing mattered anymore.

Two rescuers were approaching the tent, flanking a young teenage girl. As they drew nearer, Taylan's breath caught in her throat. The girl had been badly beaten. Both her eyes were purple and swollen and dried blood crusted her lips.

Taylan had a feeling she knew who this was. When the trio reached the tent, she said, "Hannah?"

The girl turned at the sound of the name but then she shook her head violently.

Confused, Taylan moved aside as the three entered the little hospital. Perhaps the Crusaders had beaten another child as well as the one who had helped her kids.

"Hannah!" Patrin cried out. "You're okay! I was so worried about you."

He got up from his cot—his drip had been removed earlier in the day—and ran to the girl's side.

"Hey, back to bed," a rescuer warned. "This girl needs treatment. You can see her later."

The girl gave Patrin a small smile before she was taken behind a screen.

Taylan walked over to her son and helped him back into bed. "So that *is* Hannah?"

"Uh huh," he replied, slipping his feet under the covers. "That's her."

"That's funny. She seemed angry when I said her name."

"Ohhh! It isn't her real name. She might have been angry you used it. The Crusaders gave us different ones. I don't know what her real name is."

She tucked him in and kissed his forehead. She didn't ask him what name his captors had forced him to use. She didn't want to know. Just imagining what her kids had endured was painful.

She had to focus on the future. She didn't have any idea

what to do. She'd never allowed herself the luxury of imagining life after finding her kids. When the EAC invaded they were living in a rental, so they didn't have a home to return to. Her economic situation hadn't improved during the war either, but maybe Arthur or Jonte would lend her the money for a deposit and first month's rent. Or perhaps she could squat somewhere until she got a job. There was plenty of abandoned housing in West BI. She would just have to figure something out.

She smiled wryly as she recalled Arthur's belief that Lancelot was her ancestor. Who would have thought a descendant of a Knight of the Round Table would fall so low?

HANNAH'S real name was Carys and she was from West BI. Taylan thanked her so many times for keeping her children alive during the long march through the desert, she seemed to be getting embarrassed. She flushed as she peered through the slits of her puffy eyes. "I didn't do anything special," she insisted. "Anyone would have done the same. I only wish I could have helped more of them."

Survivor's guilt.

Taylan knew how that felt. Every firefight she'd taken part in where Marines died, she'd asked herself why them and not her. "You did everything you could. Don't ever think you could have done more. None of what happened was your fault. Do your parents know you're okay? Has anyone been in contact with them yet?"

Carys's head fell and she replied quietly, "I don't know. No one's said anything."

"I'll find out for you." She comm'd Ricci.

He seemed flustered when he answered, "The BI authorities are working on contacting all the families. As soon as I hear anything I'll let Carys know."

He cut the comm.

Carys's head sank further and she began to weep. Taylan put her arms around her. She couldn't imagine the ordeal the girl had endured, and now she faced the possibility of never being reunited with her family. Many BI citizens had died during and after the invasion.

The tent flap lifted and Arthur appeared. "Could I speak to you please, Taylan?"

His tone implied he wanted to speak in private. She joined him at the entrance.

"There's been a change of plan," he said quietly. "You and I are to return to Sydney the day after tomorrow and from there we'll fly to the *Dauntless*."

"No way!" she whispered back. "Patrin and Kayla aren't well enough to go on a trip like that so soon."

"The doctor has stated they'll be fine by then."

She looked at her kids. Aside from their sunburn, they did seem remarkably unaffected by their experience. But that was only their physical state. Who knew what mental effects they would suffer and for how long? "I don't like the idea of moving them, especially not to a freaking starship. If they're going to go anywhere, it should be home, back to West BI. Why does the Alliance even want me at this meeting? It doesn't make any sense."

"It's complicated to explain. I advise you to come so you can hear it in person. And," he added, "you'll be able to see Major Wright again."

"Wright?" Her stomach clenched. "Why should I care about seeing him?"

Arthur gave her a knowing look. "You spoke about TJ many times as we were driving through the desert. When you weren't talking about your children, you were talking about him."

"Was I? I don't remember that."

Now it was her turn to blush.

Arthur said softly, touching her arm, "Love is not shameful."

To her utter embarrassment, Taylan felt herself turn redder.

"In my time," Arthur continued, "people of my class couldn't marry for love. Only peasants had that luxury, and even then not always. People like me had to marry for reasons of state, money, power, or influence. Nevertheless, I loved my queen with my whole heart. I never regretted making her my wife, despite everything that happened between us."

Taylan winced, feeling somehow responsible for her supposed ancestor's adulterous affair with Guinevere.

"You should take your chances where you find them," said Arthur. "You deserve to be loved. Though your language is often foul, you have a pure heart."

The conversation was getting entirely too uncomfortable.

"All right," she said, "I'll go with you to the *Dauntless*. But after that it's straight back home."

"Are we going home soon?" Kayla asked. Her cot was nearer than Patrin's and she'd obviously been earwigging.

"Not just yet," Taylan replied, raising her voice. "We have to go to a starship first. How does that sound?"

Kayla turned her widened eyes to her brother, who looked equally surprised.

"A starship?" Patrin asked. "I'd love to go to a starship!"

20

They had put Taylan and her kids in a two-bedroom suite. Why there *was* a two-bedroom suite on a military ship, she had no idea. Maybe the rooms were for visiting dignitaries. The Alliance certainly seemed to be treating her like a dignitary. Someone had sent a form asking her to list requirements for her stay. She'd taken full advantage, requesting clothes, snacks, and toys for Patrin and Kayla. They had nothing to wear except the rags they were in when she found them.

It was bizarre. Why was the BA treating her so well?

And why was it building the *Dauntless*, a state-of-the-art, FTL battleship? The war with the EAC was over and Ua Talman had begun asteroid mining, abandoning most of his Earth-based operations.

The *Dauntless* was still under construction. Their escorted walk to their suite from the shuttle had been accompanied by the sounds of power tools. Even now she could feel vibrations under her feet. Why was the BA holding a meeting aboard an incomplete ship?

The door chime sounded. When Taylan opened it, a guard stood outside. "I am to escort you to the meeting, ma'am."

"Is it time already?"

She told Patrin and Kayla to choose something to bring with them. Kayla grabbed an interface—she'd been watching children's shows—but Patrin picked up some paper and pencils. It hurt Taylan to see the Crusaders' influence on him but she bit her tongue. If knowing how to write and draw by hand were the only lasting effects of his time among the cultists, he would be lucky.

"Umm..." the guard hesitated as the children came to the door.

"What?" Taylan asked. "You can't expect me to leave them here by themselves."

He relented and they followed him along the passageway. When they arrived at the meeting room, another guard stood at the entrance. This one was more forthright. As Taylan was about to step into the room, she blocked the way. "Apologies, ma'am, there's been a mistake. If you would please wait a moment..."

She murmured into her comm.

Taylan said, "If you think I'm leaving my kids with a babysitter, think again."

The guard locked eyes with her.

"Either all of us or none of us go in there," she went on, "and you can explain my absence to whatever jumped-up official it was who insisted I came here."

The guard continued mouthing the soft conversation she was having via her implant. Then, with a reluctant look, she stepped aside.

Most of the seats around the table were already filled. Taylan spotted the only set of three empty ones together and headed for them, ignoring the attention Patrin and Kayla were drawing.

Seriously, what did the Alliance expect her to do? Abandon them to some stranger after she'd nearly lost them forever?

She settled Patrin into a seat with his paper and pencils, but Kayla insisted on sitting on her lap. It was only to be expected.

Taylan lifted her gaze and found the other attendees still watching her. She met each pair of eyes frankly with a blank stare. She knew most of the people: Colbourn, who was looking at her as though she'd crawled out from under a rock; Lieutenant-General Carol, who broke eye contact quickly; three men she didn't recognize but clearly thought she should; a petite, short-haired woman smiling kindly at her, and next to her a man Taylan had never met but knew instantly—Lorcan Ua Talman. He looked older than she remembered from his pictures in the media.

Sitting alone with an empty seat to each side of her was a woman who instantly filled her with hatred and disgust: Kala Orr. This was the person who was responsible for everything her children had gone through, and if they'd died their blood would have been on her hands. It was all Taylan could do to not launch herself over the table and strangle the woman. And to think she'd once stopped Arthur from killing her.

Of all the people present, Orr was the only one ignoring her.

As if summoned by her thoughts, the king stepped into the room. He raised a hand in greeting before scanning for somewhere to sit. The only remaining spaces were next to Orr and Kayla's chair, which was technically empty. He walked around the table to sit beside Taylan.

Then Wright walked in.

All the anger and revulsion she'd been feeling about Kala Orr melted away. His smile filled her with warmth. Colbourn gave a loud cough, diverting the major's attention. His face fell, and he pulled out a chair next to Orr before sitting down.

"I believe everyone has arrived?" asked one of the important-looking men.

The man beside him nodded.

"Excellent. We won't bother with introductions. I believe most of us are known to each other and if we aren't, so much the better. Needless to say, nothing of what is discussed here is to be mentioned again to anyone except those present."

He continued, "I'll get straight to the point. Our planet is under threat. Recent events have revealed the existence of aliens who have been manipulating humankind for their benefit and entertainment. The scale of their interference and the resulting loss of life is impossible to estimate, but needless to say we cannot allow this situation to continue. As many of you know, this ship and its crew will address this threat. When she is complete and ready for action, the *Dauntless* will voyage beyond the heliosphere on an exploratory mission. For the first time in human history, men and women will venture into interstellar space. The need to increase our knowledge of life outside our Solar System is vital and urgent. That is beyond question. All we have to decide here today are the details."

Taylan had guessed the meeting might be something to do with the revelation that Merlin and Morgan had been playing a game with human lives, and the game wasn't over. She'd told Wright the Alliance wouldn't—couldn't—ignore the ongoing menace to human civilization.

The only thing that puzzled her was why *she* was here. Maybe they wanted to ask her about her experiences with the aliens, though she hadn't spent much time with either of them. Wright and Arthur were the people to talk to about Merlin, and Orr probably knew Morgan best of any of them.

"I would like to take this opportunity to thank Ua Talman," said the official, "without whose support the fitting of the *Dauntless* with her FTL engine would have been impossible."

Talman waved a hand dismissively. "No need for any

thanks. My motives aren't entirely selfless. The advancement of humanity has always been my aim, and hopefully the facts gleaned on this mission will help ensure the safety of my colony ships when they depart."

"Nevertheless, I acknowledge your generosity. Now, let's get on to the mission participants. Naturally, the ship will be crewed by our finest Marines, but a question hangs over who else should go along."

Taylan's ears pricked up.

"Consultation with King Arthur has informed our decision-making in this area. Though I don't fully understand why, it seems that individuals who played a role in the events involving Merlin and Morgan are significant. He feels these people should be included in the mission, that they may still have a part to play."

He meant Arthur's theory about patterns.

"If you mean me," Orr spat, "my participation is out of the question. I'm *not* leaving Earth. I have a realm to rule, though you've all done your best to rip it from me."

"Let's not mince words," said the official. "You are ruling in name only and only by the consent of the Alliance, which," he added menacingly, "could be revoked at any time."

"I'd like to see you try it," Orr retorted. "My people would rise up and revolt. Then what would happen to your precious Alliance?"

"And I'd like to remind you," Lorcan countered, "that I have evidence your son is responsible for the deaths of sixteen men and women, killed by the bomb blast he engineered on the *Bres*. Sixteen highly skilled, intelligent individuals much loved and missed by their families. It was only by the merest chance the life of my colleague, whose knowledge will be invaluable on this trip, was saved."

"Well, Lorcan," the petite woman demurred, "I haven't decided if I'm going yet."

His words had silenced Orr, however, who merely scowled at him.

"So this is why I'm here?" Taylan asked Arthur quietly.

"Yes. I couldn't talk to you about it earlier."

"Right. Um," she raised her voice to address the room. "I can save you all some time. I'm not coming on the mission. I'll leave now so I don't hear any more details." She told Patrin to gather up his paper and pencils.

"*You* don't get a choice," said Colbourn, who sat opposite.

"I'm sorry?!"

"Perhaps you didn't hear me? Your cooperation isn't optional. You've been closely involved since the beginning and you have no good reason to refuse, so—"

"In case you hadn't noticed, I have two very good reasons." She placed a hand on her children's heads. "If you think I'm going to abandon—"

"I'm sure you can find someone reliable to care for them while you're gone."

Taylan was speechless. She'd always known Colbourn was a cold-hearted bitch, but this was beyond the pale.

"My friend's objections are valid," said Arthur. "We should try to find a compromise. Taylan, what if Patrin and Kayla come with us?"

"Sir," Colbourn interrupted, "I am afraid you misunderstand. It is quite normal now for parents to have others care for their children for extended periods while they work. Things are different from how they were in your time."

Arthur looked at Taylan, Patrin, and Kayla. "I don't believe they are."

She got up. "I've heard enough. Arthur, don't take this personally. I'm grateful for your help in finding my kids, and maybe there is something in your theory about patterns, but this isn't for me."

"Sit down!" Colbourn exclaimed. "No one gave you permission to leave."

What *was* the brigadier on?

"I don't need anyone's permission." Taylan took each of her children's hands and began to edge around the outside of the table.

"No need to be hasty," said the official. "Perhaps we could discuss this further."

"There isn't anything to discuss. I'm sorry. I hope the mission is a success."

"Sit down," Colbourn repeated. When Taylan ignored her, she added, "If you refuse to do your duty there will be repercussions."

The brigadier seemed the only person who was pitching a fit. Most of the other attendees appeared confused. Orr looked disdainful. Arthur appeared sad and disappointed. As she passed Ua Talman, he leaned back as if to talk to her, but he actually spoke to Patrin. "Can I see your drawing, son?"

He held up the paper, showing a story he'd been writing, and Talman's eyebrows rose. "You can write by hand? What a clever boy. What's your name?"

Patrin proudly gave his full name. The older man nodded, and Taylan moved on.

A look passed between her and Wright before she left. He didn't mind what she was doing.

He understood.

21

———

Taylan took a final look at Patrin and Kayla as they lay sleeping in their beds. They'd dropped off within minutes of her beginning to read them a bedtime story. They might be medically healthy according to the Australian doctor, but their little bodies and minds would take a long time to recover from their experiences with the Crusaders. They were both eating like horses and sleeping for hours on end, which made her glad and sad.

As to the mental effects of their ordeal, it might take years for them to go away, especially for Patrin. He hadn't only suffered hardship, fear, and deprivation, he'd borne the responsibility of protecting Kayla and keeping her alive. He acted far older than he was, caring for his sister like a parent not a brother.

She closed the bedroom door and sighed. Her children had a long road ahead of them. Perhaps they would always bear the scars of what they'd endured, but they were safe at last.

No one had come to the suite since she'd left the meeting. She supposed they were all busy with their discussions and arrangements. Tomorrow, a shuttle to take her and her kids back to Earth. With luck, it would go to the BI. If they were returned to Sydney she would need money for tickets to go home.

She was making some tea and thinking she might as well get an early night too when the door chime rang. It was Major Wright, holding a bottle of wine in one hand, two glasses in the other, and a large box under one arm.

Surprised, she blurted, "How did you press the button?"

He smiled. "With my nose. Is this bad timing? Only I didn't think it was fair you were missing out on the party."

"Party? They're having a party and I wasn't invited? That figures." She stepped to one side to give him room to come in. "Colbourn must have crossed my name off the invitation list."

She took the bottle and glasses from him and put them on the coffee table.

"You're definitely not in her good books," said Wright.

"Was I ever?"

He considered. "No." He put the box down and opened it. "I brought you a present."

"Boots!"

The cat looked up at her and miaowed. She gathered him into her arms. He seemed to remember her as he began to purr. "I missed you." After cuddling him, she put him down and he trotted off to explore the suite.

She hugged Wright. "Thanks for looking after him. Are you sure you don't want him to come with you on your mission?"

"I don't think interstellar space is any place for a cat. He'll be happier with you and your kids."

"I won't argue with you. Patrin and Kayla will love him. Thanks for coming to see me. Are you sure you won't be missed at the party? I don't want you to get in trouble."

"No, it's fine. I made the rounds and had a couple of conversations with dignitaries before slipping out. As long as I showed my face no one will complain. I'm not that important.

Poor Arthur, though. The Sea Lord is making him explain jousting."

"The Sea Lord was one of the men at the meeting, right?" she asked. She didn't know the man's name but she didn't want to appear ignorant.

"Yes, and the Chief of Defence, Admiral York, and the new Prime Minister. You didn't recognize her?"

"I haven't been paying attention to the news." She realized they were still standing awkwardly. She gestured. "Sit down."

They sat on opposing sides of the corner sofa and he poured wine into the glasses.

"It's good to see you again," he said, handing her a glass. "How are your children doing?"

She grimaced. "As well as can be expected. I couldn't have found them without Arthur's help. And he didn't only help me find them, he saved our lives."

"Really? What happened?"

Regretting mentioning the subject, she replied, "I don't want to talk about it right now. What's been happening with you?"

"Marine stuff. You know the kind of thing. It's quieter now the war's over but things are getting more complicated. There's a lot of diplomacy going on and not much action. I was pulled from my duties on the *Resolute* and stuck back into the political shenanigans with Arthur and Kala Orr. It's not my cup of tea. I miss the *Resolute*. Hey, have you seen Abacha?"

"No. Is he here?"

"He is. I'll find him for you before you leave so you can say hi. He's here because Arthur thinks he should go on the mission."

"Why on Earth does he think that?"

"You heard what the Sea Lord was saying at the meeting. Arthur believes the people involved in what happened with Merlin and Morgan are connected somehow. He thinks we have parts to play in freeing humans from alien influence. Abacha's here because he's associated with you."

"So just because he's my friend?"

"Taylan, you don't understand. According to Arthur, *you're* integral to this whole thing. Do you know he thinks you're descended from Lancelot?"

She laughed. "Yes, he told me. Crazy, right?"

He didn't answer.

"Don't tell me you believe him."

"I'm not as skeptical as I was. Merlin told me himself about the patterns he followed to play his 'game', though he admitted he didn't fully understand or see all of them. At the time I thought he was bullshitting, but there was that moment when all of us came together—Arthur, Orr, Morgan, Merlin, me, you, Colbourn—the people who had been involved from the beginning when I carried Arthur from the cave. Merlin announced an outcome was imminent then Arthur cut off his head. That was one hell of an outcome. When you look back at how things played out, defeating Orr and winning back the Isles, you have to admit—"

"I'm not going on the mission," Taylan said abruptly, suddenly fearful of the reason he'd come here.

He held up a hand. "I never thought you would. You won't hear any argument from me."

"I have other responsibilities now."

"I know. No reasonable person would expect you to agree to it."

She sipped wine. "No one except Colbourn, who might not count as reasonable."

"I'm sorry she had a go at you. She's very single-minded."

Taylan could think of more colorful terms to describe the brigadier, but she knew Wright had a soft spot for her so she held her tongue.

Her interface bleeped, announcing she received a message.

"Excuse me a sec." She picked it up from the tabletop, wondering what it could be. The net had only been re-established on the BI for a short while and all the old data had been lost. She'd opened an account but no one knew about it yet.

"Oh!" she softly exclaimed as she read the mail.

"What is it?"

"That's odd." She read the message again and then clicked on the link. She read the information twice. "Holy shit! This has to be a mistake."

"What?"

Bemused, she placed her interface back on the table. "A small fortune has been deposited in my bank account. It must be a glitch, with all the systems starting up again and everything. I'll sort it out when I get back home."

"I don't think it's a mistake. Congratulations."

"It's real?!"

"I think it may be."

"How do you know? Was it Arthur? The Alliance gave him a shit ton of money. He probably doesn't know what to do with it."

"Actually, I think it was Ua Talman. He was singing your son's praises at the party, saying how no one teaches kids how to hand write anything anymore. It's a dying art, and so on. I reckon he must have guessed you're not exactly rolling in money right now and wanted to help you out."

"Ha! If only he knew it was Crusaders who taught Patrin how to do that. Don't let him know, will you? He might take the money back."

"Don't worry. I won't say a dword."

"What a relief! I was worried about finding somewhere to live and getting a job. It's chaos in West BI at the moment. Now, if I'm careful, that's me and the kids set up for the next couple of decades. I'll have to find Talman and thank him."

"You might get a chance tomorrow before he leaves. He isn't

coming on the mission, though his colleague, Iolani Hale is. She told me she's made her mind up to come along."

"Is that the woman who was with him at the meeting? She seemed nice."

"She's lovely. You would like her. Arthur thinks she's significant in the pattern too, due to the way she survived the bomb blast on the *Bres*."

"What happened?"

"She was blown into an open elevator and the doors shut just before the section lost power. All the ship's elevators automatically pressure seal in emergencies. When Arthur found out about Talman's involvement in the war and Hale's story, he asked to meet her. She's an expert on living organisms. He reckons she might help us understand the aliens."

Taylan frowned. "Arthur is such a big, fat liar. He told me no one was telling him anything about what was going on, but in fact he's been scheming behind the scenes all along."

"It's more complicated than that. The Alliance began work on the *Dauntless* months ago. It was only after the incident with Merlin the decision was taken to replace her engine with an FTL drive and explore interstellar space. Arthur tried to offer his advice but all the higher-ups ignored him. Then he pulled his stunt and disappeared off to Australia with you. *That* made them pay attention. They want and need their ancient king of the Britannic Isles. There's definitely more to Arthur than meets the eye, especially now he isn't under Merlin's influence anymore."

Wright drank his wine and relaxed in his seat as they shared a comfortable silence until Taylan noticed something new about the major. "Your uniform is different. Have you been promoted?"

"No, this is my dress uniform, for public occasions. You had one too, remember?"

She shook her head.

He rolled his eyes, and she chuckled. After a pause, she said, "You know, I don't think I've ever seen you out of uniform."

He spread his arms across the back of his seat and replied gallantly, "That can always be arranged."

"Okay."

He laughed, but when her expression remained serious he stopped. His eyebrows popped up. "Taylan, I didn't come here expecting—"

"I know."

"I only thought it would be good to chat and catch—"

"I know."

The atmosphere turned tense.

She gathered a breath. "The way this would usually work is we would go out to dinner a few times and get to know each other. Maybe you would buy me flowers. But tomorrow I'm returning to the surface and you'll stay here to prepare for the mission. Then you'll be gone for who knows how long." She swallowed. "I might never see you again."

He put down his glass. He held her gaze for some moments before moving around to her side of the sofa and putting his arm around her. She rested her head on his shoulder and closed her eyes. The trials of the last few days faded from her mind. All the weeks and months of despair and self-hatred were forgotten, and it was just her and Wright and her children finally safe.

"You seem different too," he murmured.

"Do I?"

"Yes. It's like you're complete now."

It wasn't true, but she didn't argue.

He kissed her.

At some point during the night, she whispered, "Don't go on the mission. Resign. Stay with me."

He whispered back, "I can't."

When she woke in the morning he was gone. She didn't blame him. It was better this way.

Her interface had moved from the lounge to her bedside table overnight. She reached out for it.

He'd left her a message: *Don't wait for me.*

She sat up and pulled on her robe. Pushing back the covers, she swung her legs over the side of the bed, but she couldn't seem to go any farther.

A while later, Patrin opened the door, tousle-haired and sleepy-eyed.

When he saw her, he hesitated. "Mam, what's wrong? Are you sad you found us?"

"God, no! Why would you think that?"

"Why are you crying?"

She wiped her eyes. "No reason. Come here. Let me give you a hug."

PART II

22

____

Wright stared down at his breakfast. The bagel sat untouched on its plate and his mug of black coffee was full to the brim. He had no appetite. Just the thought of putting the food or drink to his lips made him want to vomit.

For some reason he didn't quite understand, he felt like it was his eighteenth birthday again. He was walking up the garden path of his home, arriving home from school. It had been a good day. His friends had bought him presents and played a few harmless pranks on the birthday boy. He'd enjoyed the attention and sense of comradeship from the people he'd known since he was eleven or even younger. He'd been on a high, full of the excitement of coming of age, of becoming an adult in the eyes of society.

During school hours he managed to forget the coldness at home. He wasn't sure how old he'd been when he'd realized his parents didn't want him, let alone love him, but he'd known it most of his childhood. Unlike his friends' parents, they were never happy to see him or interested in what he did. He was always fed and clothed and they never hit him or shouted at him, but neither was there ever any warmth or affection from them. His presence was tolerated and that was it.

So when he got home from school that day he really should have expected the pile of his belongings sitting outside his parents' front door. They hadn't given him any warning, but the writing had been on the wall for years. He should have seen it coming. They no longer had any legal responsibility for his welfare. The severing of their relationship was effective immediately.

It took him a couple of minutes to get over the shock. After that, he didn't even bother ringing the doorbell—he'd never been allowed a key. Instead, he'd called his best friend and explained the situation, embarrassed and hurt. His friend's parents had put him up for the remainder of the school year. Tactful and kind, they'd never brought up the subject of his mother and father's behavior.

And he'd never mentioned it, not to them or anyone else, not once in the years that had passed. He always told people his parents were dead. To him, they were.

His friend's parents had helped him with the legal side of things so he wouldn't have to rely on his parents' financial support for further study, but in the end he'd applied for Royal Marines officer training. He hadn't wanted to impose on the kindness of strangers any longer, and he figured that if his real family didn't want him, he would find another one in his work. As the saying goes, the rest was history.

Ancient history.

So why was that gut-wrenching, frantic feeling back again?

The sound of chair legs scraping on tile drew him back to the present. He looked up.

Arthur was sitting down opposite him. "Did you see Taylan last night?"

Wright nodded.

"Did you try to persuade her to come on the mission?"

"No! Why would I do that?"

"I believe her presence may be vital."

Wright stared at him. "She has two kids to look after. You seriously believe she would even consider setting off into interstellar space? I don't understand why she was even asked to come here. What kind of parent would abandon their children?"

He breathed in sharply. Was *that* where the feeling was coming from? When he was a kid, his parents would have abandoned him in a heartbeat, given the chance.

"As I said at the meeting," Arthur countered, "perhaps her children could come too."

"No, it doesn't work like that." Wright imagined the disparaging comments from BA military higher-ups about crèches and nursemaids. "Even if Taylan were to consider the idea, which I'm sure she wouldn't, the *Dauntless* is a military vessel embarking on a military mission. It's far too dangerous a place for children. Taking them with us would be entirely against protocol."

He sighed and rested his forehead on his fingertips.

"Is something wrong, TJ?"

"I'm not feeling great, that's all."

He could feel Arthur watching him. They sat in silence, the bustle and hum of the mess going on around them.

"You will miss Taylan when we leave," Arthur said softly.

Wright didn't answer. He was barely keeping it together as it was.

"Are you considering not coming on the mission too?" Arthur asked.

"No. I must. The future of humanity is under threat and the Alliance is right to attempt to do something about it. I must play my part." He almost added, *This is what I do. It's who I am.* But he wasn't sure that was true anymore.

Another silence stretched out.

Wright's bagel and cooling coffee occupied his vision.

Arthur's chair scraped the floor again as he stood up, and then the man's large hand clapped down on his shoulder. "You must do what you feel is right, TJ. That's all any of us can do."

It was as if the king had heard what he was thinking.

His shadow passed over Wright as he walked away.

A second later...

"Major."

Colbourn had arrived and was staring down at him pensively. "Kala Orr is being difficult again. We're concerned that if she returns to the surface she might do something stupid, so she'll remain here until we're ready to leave."

Wright tensed as he predicted what was coming next.

"You're in charge of keeping her under control until we're underway."

He inwardly groaned. "Yes, Brigadier."

Her stare hardened. "Don't mope, man. It doesn't suit you." She left.

He had a lot of respect for Colbourn, but sometimes he ached to punch her in the face.

23

Kala Orr crouched in the shadows near the airlock. Her posture was so undignified she felt sickened. How had things come to this? That she, Dwyr Orr, was forced to hide like a common fugitive? It was as if *she* had done something wrong, not the vile people who now felt as though they had the right to control her life.

She should never have agreed to come here. She hated this ship and everything it stood for. The *Dauntless*. Huh! The Britannic Alliance was not dauntless, and its mission to explore interstellar space in the hope of discovering more about aliens like Merlin and Morgan was arrogant and foolish.

The Alliance had only succeeded in winning back the BI through a set of odd coincidences. The pattern Arthur spoke of was nonsense. Entities like Morgan exercised control, and if they had been playing with human lives, so what? Hopefully they would not return for a very long time, long after she and Perran were dead.

She had a kingdom to rule, and the Alliance was determined to keep her from it. *That* was the real reason for this mission. They wanted to separate her from Perran. With her out of the way, they could do as they pleased with the remaining EAC lands. Perran was too young and weak to defy them. By the time she returned, it would all be over.

She couldn't let that happen. She had to return to Earth. With Arthur gone, it shouldn't be too hard to push back all the Alliance initiatives and fight for her people and their way of life.

Footsteps echoed down the passageway. The party about to disembark was arriving.

She peeked out.

Two guards appeared around a bend in the corridor.

If the main group was sufficiently far away…

She watched from the shadows as the first guard opened the airlock. The two stepped inside.

A *clunk* resounded as the farther hatch was opened.

Now was her chance. She threw a glance up the passageway. It was empty, though the footsteps and voices were growing louder.

She ran into the airlock. Her foot caught on the lip of the hatch and she came down heavily on her knees and right wrist, the impact jarring up to her shoulder. In another second she was up and running into the shuttle.

One of the soldiers was suddenly in her way. They collided and she bounced backward, almost falling again.

"Sorry, ma'am," the man said, confused. "I didn't see you."

He didn't know she wasn't supposed to be here.

"Be more careful next time," she snapped before stepping around him and into the passenger cabin.

Where to hide?

Ugh. She hated stooping to this ridiculous behavior. But if she could only make it to Earth, once she was out in public in the spaceport, the Alliance wouldn't dare drag her away against her will. Tensions were high and the BA couldn't risk inciting insurrection.

The shuttle would be full. More dignitaries had been visiting the *Dauntless* than had been present at the meeting. There was no point in trying to sneak under some seats or into one of the larger lockers. She would soon be discovered.

The noise of approaching people burst from behind her. They'd reached the airlock!

She dashed down the aisle. There was nothing for it. She would have to hide in the restroom. Her stomach churning with loathing, she slipped into the small room and locked the door.

"Yes, she's a beautiful ship," said a booming male voice. "I'm sad to leave her. Wish I was going on the mission myself, but sadly my days of active service are over."

It was the Sea Lord, Fox. The odious man was a dreadful bore. He had to be subjecting a lesser official to his self-important monologue.

"Of course, as soon as we heard about the presence of aliens on Earth for centuries interfering in human affairs, my mind immediately sprang to the *Dauntless*. She was always intended for stealth operations. The cloaking equipment we trialed on the *Gallant* was a part of her original design—what's that?"

Someone else spoke, but too quietly for Kala to make out what they said.

"Yes, yes, all right," said Fox impatiently.

It was probably someone telling him to fasten his seatbelt because as he replied, a vibration had started up beneath Kala's feet. The shuttle engine had ignited. Everyone was aboard and the hatch must have been shut.

She was nearly on her way.

"And the very latest in armaments, naturally," Fox went on. "Though I can't tell you anything about *that* of course. The war might be over and the *Dauntless* might be leaving the Solar System for a while, but we can't be too careful. You never know when the Alliance might be called upon to save the day once more."

Kala's fingernails dug into her palms as she tightened her hands into fists.

Save the day?

The man's smugness was beyond words. The BA hadn't saved the day. It had torn her from her people and intended to make her son a puppet, depriving millions of the right to live their lives as they chose.

Fox droned on.

What was taking so long? The shuttle should have left by now.

Fox abruptly stopped speaking. At the same time, other voices in the passenger cabin grew quieter. They'd been chattering but a hush descended.

What was going on?

Rap, rap, rap!

The loud knocking at the restroom door made her jump.

She was still.

"Open up," a male voice ordered.

It sounded familiar. Was it—?

The lock disengaged and the door opened.

Major Wright stood in the doorway with a face like thunder. "Come with me."

There was no *Dwyr*, no *ma'am*, no deference at all. The man had no idea of the respect she deserved. She would never forget how he had held her down and threatened her after she'd tried to kill his stupid cat.

"I will not!"

He strode in, twisted her arm up her back, and forced her out into the cabin.

"Let go of me!" she yelled. "You have no right to lay hands

on me. Ow! You're hurting me! You're assaulting the Dwyr. I won't stand for it, I'll..."

All the passengers watched as the major frogmarched her down the aisle. The humiliation was too much to bear. Then she saw Taylan Ellis and her horrible children. How come *she*, a nobody, was allowed to refuse to join the stupid mission while the Dwyr was not?

The major slowed down briefly as he passed Ellis, but then pushed harder, making her walk faster until they were through the airlock and back aboard the *Dauntless*.

As she was urged down the passageway, the airlock hatch clanked closed behind them. Only then did the major's pressure on her arm ease. He released her, and she spun to face him before slapping him hard across the cheek.

"How *dare* you manhandle me! Never touch me again, or I'll—"

He drove his forearm into her throat, thrusting her against the wall and knocking the back of her head into it. Outraged, she was about to scream at him, but his arm pressed into her windpipe so hard she couldn't speak.

"Listen to me," he hissed, his eyes full of hatred and rage. "We'll be aboard this ship a long time, and I'm the poor bastard in charge of you while you're here. Put one more step out of line, make one more attempt to leave, and I'll space you. No question. I don't care what Arthur says. The Alliance doesn't need you. The BI doesn't need you. No one will care if you don't return from this mission. Do you understand me?"

She wanted to defy him. She wanted to threaten him. But from the look on his face she was in no doubt he meant every word he'd said. She had no choice except to nod in reply.

He stepped back and his arm dropped to his side.

She rubbed her throat, expecting him to tell her to return to her cabin or give her another order. But he walked off as if she no longer existed.

She watched him leave.

Do you really think you can tell me what to do, Major Wright? I might have lost my son and my kingdom, but I still have some fight left in me. I have nothing left to lose now. You'd better watch your back.

24

———

A holo of the local galactic sector hung in the air in the briefing room. The lights had been dimmed to near-darkness in order to make the star systems clearly visible. Wright stared, unseeing, at the display.

Lieutenant-General Carol had been droning on for half an hour about the mission, going over facts everyone knew already. The man loved the sound of his own voice. Spending the next who knew how many months in the man's company promised to be challenging.

Wright recalled the crew of the *Resolute.* What a contrast. If only Ford, Jeong, and the others were here it might make the trip more bearable. Even Krol would be a pleasure to have aboard compared to Carol, Colbourn and, worst of all, Kala Orr. Just the sight of the woman made his blood boil.

"So as you know," Carol said, "we aren't heading for the obvious target, Alpha Centauri. Probe data indicates no atmosphere on any of the planets of Proxima Centauri or the binary system, so it's a waste of time."

Iolani Hale gave a loud cough.

"Instead," Carol continued, "we're—"

"Pardon me," said Hale. "I'd like to say something."

The lieutenant-general's face twisted in annoyance, as if he was not used to being interrupted. He laid down the pointer he'd been using to indicate the stars he mentioned. "Please be my guest, Ms Hale."

A trace of sarcasm had crept into his tone, but the scientist either didn't notice or didn't care. She rose to her feet. "I'd like my objection to the choice of destination for this mission to go on the record. I expressed my concerns and reasoning when the decision was made, but my opinion was disregarded."

Carol said, "The Alliance must take *all* opinions into account when deciding where to allocate its resources and funding. I'm sure your expertise and experience is valued and appreciated, nevertheless—"

"There's no reason to suppose these aliens aren't living on an Alpha Centaurian planet," Hale interrupted. "We have anecdotal evidence that they're able to survive in the vacuum of space. They don't need a breathable atmosphere. And if they're able to change their physical state from a solid to a gas at will, they probably aren't bound by gravity either. They could easily exist on a high-g planet, or even a moon or asteroid."

"In which case," said Carol, "they could be anywhere. So by your own logic it really doesn't matter where we go."

Wright wasn't entirely up to speed on their destination. All he knew was the planet was the nearest that could sustain life but not human life, according to the data from Ua Talman's probes.

He didn't know Carol particularly well, but he knew him well enough to be confident the officer didn't have the first idea of what he was talking about. He knew nothing about xenoplanets or extraterrestrial organisms. He'd been given the mission destination and that was where he was going, come hell or high water. Hale was wasting her time. She just didn't know it yet.

Wright asked, "Can you tell us any more about what you've figured out about the aliens?"

Carol shot him an angry look. Wright was siding with the civilian and against his superior officer, but he didn't care.

Looking somewhat mollified, Hale replied, "Well, it's all supposition until I get the chance to study them properly, but one thing we should bear in mind is they seem to be extremely long-lived."

Carol gave a snort of derision. "Thank you for your insight, but I think *everyone's* aware of that. I mean, they lived at least as long as Arthur."

"No, I mean *really* long lived. Kala Orr has vouched for the fact that the one we call Morgan was trapped in closed cave systems for thousands of years. That's right, isn't it?" Hale addressed the question to Orr, who had been sitting with her arms folded over her chest, gazing sourly at the proceedings.

"That's *Dwyr* Orr to *you*," was all she said in reply.

"Assuming Orr is correct," Hale went on sweetly, "the only explanation I can think of for Morgan surviving and tolerating those conditions is that to *her*, or *it*, thousands of Earth years isn't a long time at all. Maybe her experience of the time passing was equivalent to our experience of a few hours or days, though, as I said, that's supposition. I'd rather not say any more at the moment. I don't want to prejudice impressions of these creatures if we ever encounter them, and I'm still going over the information we have on them."

"Your input is much appreciated," said Carol. "If I might continue?"

Hale sat down.

Carol re-started his droning. Wright faded out, turning his attention to the attendees. Everyone of officer rank was here including Corporal Abacha as well as civilians Hale, Arthur, and Orr. He was glad Abacha was coming along. He would have to ask him if he'd seen Taylan before she left.

The sight of her in the shuttle cabin sprang into his mind like an ember spitting from a fire. He'd hoped he would be able to get through the day of her departure without seeing her again, but Orr had put paid to that with her stupid antics.

A bolt of agony and regret had passed through him. His only consolation was he'd been able to tell Taylan didn't hate him for sneaking out without saying goodbye. She'd seemed to understand it would have been unbearable. It hadn't made seeing her again any less painful.

Carol was chuckling, though his audience didn't share his amusement. "Of course, we might not be going anywhere. The engine testing is going well, with no major hiccups. However, it won't be until after the final check in two weeks we'll know for sure the mission will go ahead according to schedule. All non-essential personnel will wait aboard the shuttles while the test run takes place. You'll be there a few hours and it'll be cramped, but it can't be helped. Better safe than sorry." He checked his notes. "I think that's it. Any questions?"

There was the usual pause during which Wright hoped everyone else felt the same as him and didn't want to prolong the meeting.

"Excellent," said Carol, turning off the holo. "Thank you for your time."

The lights brightened and the attendees began to stretch and get up.

Wright sat motionless, lacking the energy to move. Kala Orr strode past him, bumping his shoulder, no doubt on purpose. But he didn't respond. He didn't have the motivation to deal with her right now.

"I think she has it in for you."

He looked up. Iolani Hale was standing next to him.

"Orr?" Wright asked. "She hates my guts and the feeling's mutual."

"Well, she hates everyone, but she seems to be singling you

out in particular. She was looking daggers at you all through the meeting."

"Was she? I didn't notice. It's because I'm supposed to keep her in check during the mission."

"Oh no." Hale sat down. "Poor you. The trials of military life."

"You can say that again."

He was grateful for her friendliness. He'd spoken with Iolani a few times since she'd come aboard and had warmed to her. She was kind and gentle yet also smart and witty. Her presence would be a boon during the voyage.

"I'm glad you decided to come along," he said.

"Thanks. I'm still not sure I made the right decision. It was enough of an upheaval in my life when I was helping Lorcan with his colonization project. I never intended to accept a place on it and so never dreamed I would be leaving the Solar System one day. But I can see how I could be useful if we do ever encounter these aliens. The Alliance is already making rookie mistakes."

"You don't agree we should discount Alpha Centauri?"

"No, I don't, as I was explaining to Carol." She sighed. "But he ignored me. It's going to be an uphill battle to get them to listen."

"I don't have much influence, but I'll do what I can to support you."

Arthur appeared and straddled the chair in front of Wright so he could face them. "I don't believe we've been formally introduced," he said to Hale. "I'm—"

She burst out laughing. "I know who you are. I'm Iolani Hale." She reached out to shake his hand.

Arthur gave a satisfied smile. "I'm feeling good about our quest. We have some good people with us."

"So Taylan isn't important after all?" Wright asked.

"No, she is. She should be here, but she has a good reason

to refuse. I'm not sure what that means." The king rested his forearms on the back of his chair. "In my former life, when my country was in turmoil, crops failing in the fields and my people starving, my knights and I set out to find the Sangreal. It was only through achieving a vision of it that things would be set right again. I have a feeling this endeavor is similar."

"What was the Sangreal?" asked Iolani.

"A holy vessel. Only a perfectly pure knight could achieve it. Unfortunately, nearly all of us were not pure."

"But someone found it in the end?"

A shadow passed over Arthur's face. "Yes, but at a great cost."

25

S omeone had set up a vidscreen in the shuttle cabin so the passengers could watch the FTL test of the *Dauntless*. Tension tightened as they watched, not only due to the momentous event, but also because everyone was crammed in like sardines.

The *Dauntless* did carry shuttles and EEVs sufficient to hold her entire 200-person crew, but Carol hadn't wanted to deploy the emergency escape vessels unnecessarily. So anyone whose presence wasn't required during the test was forced to sit or stand aboard a shuttle.

It seemed a slapdash and potentially dangerous decision to Wright. Sure, if the test failed and they were unable to reboard, the shuttles could transport everyone to Earth at a pinch, though it would be an uncomfortable journey. But it seemed wrong to not do things properly from the outset. On the other hand, the entire enterprise was a departure from normality for the Alliance.

He stood at the rear of the shuttle where the aisle opened up, Abacha to his left and Iolani to his right. He felt sorry for the small woman as there was no way she would be able to see anything except the backs of everyone in front of her. Unfortunately, Kala Orr was close by, in the aisle seat of the rear row. The rest of the row was empty.

Abacha nodded at the back of her head and whispered, "Seems a bit unfair to make her come along on the mission."

"*Her*?" Wright asked. "Why?"

In the weeks following the briefing, he'd been meaning to ask Abacha if he'd managed to meet Taylan before she left, but each time he remembered he still couldn't bring himself to talk about her.

"Taking her away from her son," Abacha replied. "How long will it be before she sees him again?"

Wright turned and squinted at him. "Are you feeling okay?"

"Yeah, I'm fine, though I wish they would get this damned test over with and let us return to the ship."

"Good, you must be the only non-Crusader in existence who feels the slightest sympathy for Kala Orr. When we get back to Earth, remind me I have a used car to sell you."

Abacha shrugged. "She's still human at the end of the day, same as you and me."

"I'm not sure about that. The interrogators couldn't get a lot out of her, but she seems to think she's descended from Morgan, one of the aliens."

"She does? Could it be true?"

"I don't know. Maybe. Stick around with Arthur for a while and you'll hear some crazy stuff. I thought it was all bullshit for a long time, but after what I've seen and heard, I don't know what to think anymore. I just want it all to be over." He caught himself before he said too much. Abacha was his subordinate and he shouldn't be too familiar with him. But during their time on the *Resolute* the lines had become blurred, as had many aspects of his service.

Iolani had overheard him. She looked up and squeezed his arm in sympathy. "I'm actually a little excited now we're about to set off. I've warmed to the idea. I hope the test is successful. If it fails and they postpone or call off the mission, it's going to feel very anticlimactic."

"You don't have long to wait," said Wright, peering at the vidscreen. "The countdown is at four minutes 57 seconds." Unlike Hale, he was hoping the test failed. He wouldn't have minded if he had to return to Earth. He felt as though his time with the Royal Marines was coming to an end. If it wasn't for the need to defend human civilization against alien interference he might have resigned. As it was, he couldn't turn away while he still had duties to perform.

"I wish we were going to Proxima Centauri," Iolani said bitterly. "At ten times light speed, we could be there in about five months. Imagine that. Five months, and we could be the first human beings to set foot on an alien planet. And it isn't like life has been found at our destination. Lorcan's probes reported no signs of it. I don't know what experts the Alliance consulted when it made its decision to target an exoplanet purely because it has an atmosphere, but I wish I'd been one of them."

"I wouldn't give up on Proxima," said Wright. "You never know what might happen once we're beyond the heliosphere. Until then, when we know how well the *Dauntless* protects us from interstellar space, nothing's set in stone. It could be Proxima is the only star we'll be able to make it to before conditions force us to turn back."

"Yeah, that's going to be some day, isn't it?" Abacha commented. "When we become the first human beings to leave the Solar System. It's great they figured out instant comms before we left. I can't wait to comm my family"

It *was* remarkable that physicists had finally figured out how to use quantum entanglement to facilitate instantaneous communication, but Wright couldn't get excited about it. He wouldn't be comming anyone while on the voyage. The only person on Earth he wanted to speak to was Taylan, but he wanted her to move on with her life while he was gone. He wasn't going to get in the way of her happiness.

The noise in the cabin surged.

"They started up the thrusters," said Abacha.

Iolani stood on tiptoes and tried to peer over the heads.

The blue flame from the *Dauntless*'s thrusters shone out against the blackness of space.

"I wish Lorcan was here," said Iolani. "He would be so excited."

"Doesn't he have a live feed?" asked Abacha.

"Yes, but it isn't the same as being here," replied Iolani. "Not that I can actually *see* anything."

The *Dauntless* was moving away at a rapid speed, and the cameras constantly adjusted to keep up with its dwindling image. It was possible the ship would be out of range before she shifted to FTL flight. Despite Wright's lackluster interest that would be somewhat of a downer.

"He's worked so many years for this moment," Iolani went on. "Honestly, it's sent him crazy at times. And though we know the FTL drive works in probes, it isn't the same as using it to power a starship, right?"

The countdown on the vidscreen had reached single digits.

"Here we go," said Abacha.

"Eight," someone said.

Immediately, people began to join in. "Seven. Six."

"Five. Four," said Abacha.

"Three. Two," said Iolani.

"ONE!" the shout resounded around the cabin.

The *Dauntless* disappeared.

That was it. One second she was there on the screen, silvergray, oblong and bulky, with the warp generator protruding from her bow and with weaponry and scanners in their protective casings protruding from her hull, the next she was gone.

Stars shone from the space she'd occupied as if she'd never existed.

A hush fell.

"Did it work?" someone asked.

Yes, the FTL drive had worked. Now traveling faster than light, no light from the *Dauntless* reached them. She was now invisible to regular sight, though the spacetime warp created by the generator was detectable to scanners. It would only be while the FTL drive wasn't operating that her cloaking device would be effective, though even that was uncertain. Who knew what technological capabilities alien powers possessed?

Wright leaned back against the bulkhead and watched the starscape on the screen. They had a few hours to wait before the *Dauntless* would make her way back to pick them up. The last chance that he wouldn't be going on the mission had gone. In another couple of days they would set out. Humanity's first attempt to discover in person what lay beyond the boundaries of their star system would begin, and he would be a part of it. The knowledge left a sour taste in his mouth.

In her aisle seat, Kala Orr was weeping.

26

———

A heated debate was going on in the briefing room. Carol had invited the higher ranking officers and a few civilian passengers to discuss what was, to some attendees, an important subject: Crossing the Line. The stupid thing was, Crossing the Line referred to crossing the Earth's equator at sea, not the heliopause, where the Solar Wind gave out and interstellar space began.

The *Dauntless* was approaching the area now and Carol's idea was to mark the occasion with a similar tradition. Usually, crew who had never sailed over the equator were subjected to light hazing, such as meeting King Neptune and other silliness. Whatever equivalents Carol had thought up, Wright was in no mood for frivolities. He sat with his arms folded and waited for the meeting to be over.

"We have to think of this in terms of the Roman gods," snapped Captain Johns. For some reason, she seemed particularly invested in the proposed ceremony.

Representatives from all major branches of the military were aboard. For humanity's first step into the future of space exploration, the BI Government had felt it was best for the honor to be shared amongst those who had fought so hard and for so long to defend human civilization. Since starting out, Wright had made little effort to get to know the reps, but he recognized Major-General Bobbin of the BA Army, a Canadian woman about Colbourn's age, Royal Navy Commander Ryan Fletcher, and Group Captain Larson of the RAF.

"Makes sense to me," Fletcher commented. "Neptune was Roman, right?"

Mistakenly thinking Fletcher was talking to him Wright looked up, but the officer was addressing the room generally.

"Yes, exactly," said Carol. "Neptune was Roman. His Greek name was Poseidon."

"All right," said Fletcher. "So who does the victim have to swear fealty to in this case? Sol?"

Bobbin said, "I believe it's Sol Invictus, to be accurate."

"Sol Invictus," Fletcher echoed. "Bit of a mouthful."

"We're getting away from the main subject," said a man with a drawling accent. "Swearing allegiance is only a tiny part of the ceremony. It doesn't matter who they swear to as long as it's someone dressed up in a wig and make-up." He guffawed.

Wright didn't know his name, but he'd seen the man about the ship. It hadn't been until today he'd heard him speak. He was from one of the States, a southern one from the sound of his voice. A handful of guests from other countries had been invited to come along on the historic mission. Wright had guessed the man must be a wealthy businessman or perhaps a politician.

He overheard Larson mutter, "And what would *you* know about it?"

Considering Larson was RAF, this was a bit rich.

The group captain threw him a look, and Wright realized he must have unconsciously tutted.

"First things first," said Carol. "First we decide on the god, then we move on to the ceremonies. Agreed?"

This provoked general nods all around.

"So," said Carol. "We have Sol Invictus. I would also suggest Aurora, the goddess of dawn, as a potential candidate, and Caelus."

"Caelus!" echoed Bobbin. "God of the sky. I like it."

"Isn't Jupiter the god of the sky?" asked Fletcher. "I'm sure that's right."

"They both are," said Bobbin, "but Jupiter is the big cheese. He's already had a whole planet named after him. We should spread the love around a little."

"I was going to propose Pluto," Larson offered, "god of the underworld, considering we don't really know what we'll find on the other side. But if we're ruling out deities who already had a planet named after them."

"Pluto isn't a planet," the American interjected.

"That's up for debate," Larson countered.

"No, it isn't," said the American, "and it hasn't been for a very long time."

"As I understand it," Larson said, an edge creeping into his tone, "the status of Pluto has long been—"

"We're getting off-topic," Carol interrupted, "but we can't in all fairness dismiss gods because they have a planet named after them. Neptune is the figure used in the original Crossing-the-Line ceremony."

"Good point, Lieutenant-General," said Larson.

Wright rolled his eyes. Larson was such a brown nose, even to officers in other forces.

"So we have Sol Invictus," Carol continued, "Aurora, Caelus, and Pluto. Any more suggestions before we take a vote?"

Wright tuned out.

He would much rather be alone, or, if he had to spend time

in company, with Arthur, Abacha, and Iolani. The four of them had formed a friendship that was about the only saving grace of this wretched mission. Technically, he should have been keeping an eye on Kala Orr during the Active Shift, but she rarely left her cabin and he could hardly sit in there with her, making sure she wasn't up to no good.

What could she actually do anyway? She had no access to weapons or secure areas like the bridge. Aside from inducing disgust and hatred wherever she went, she was powerless.

"Major?"

He looked up. Carol was staring at him, and so was everyone else.

"You haven't voted," said the Lieutenant-General. "Don't you have an opinion?"

"No, I…"

Colbourn gave him a stern look.

He cleared his throat. "Er…Aurora?"

"Ah!" Carol exclaimed. "You're my man. That makes her a clear winner. Aurora it is."

"But it has to be a man," said the American. "You've gotta have a guy dressing up as a woman. You've just gotta."

"Aurora isn't a woman," Colbourn said. "She's a goddess. A female deity."

"Having a man dressing up as the opposite sex makes a mockery of the ceremony," Larson objected.

"That's the point!" the American argued. "It's supposed to be a joke."

"I'm so glad we have an expert among us," said Larson acidly. "What would we do without you?"

"It's no problem. Glad to help." The sarcasm had sailed right over the American's head.

"Yeah, like *you* know all about it," said Commander Fletcher to Larson.

"Now then," Carol said diplomatically, "all opinions are valued, especially our esteemed guests'. We have chosen our mythological figure, let's discuss the rites and rituals. Remember, we will be establishing a tradition that will be passed down through the ages. Whenever a member of the BA's military forces passes through the heliopause they will be inducted into the exclusive ranks of voyagers in interstellar space. We must think this through carefully. The actions should be symbolic yet not too serious. Any thoughts anyone?"

A barrage of suggestions erupted. Most of the attendees had an opinion on what the ceremony should entail. Carol frowned as he tried to listen but then gave up and waved his hands, trying to motion the speakers to silence.

Wright surreptitiously slid out a pocket interface and checked the time. He lifted his eyebrows and gazed around the room. Everyone was chattering, if not to Carol then to their neighbor. The meeting was descending into chaos. Small arguments were breaking out. Even Colbourn, who usually had no patience for vapid nonsense, was trying to make herself heard.

Outside the briefing room, the lower ranks were performing their duties reliably and effectively. Arthur and Iolani were probably deep in conversation somewhere. Each found the other a fascinating source of information. Iolani wanted to know all about the plants and animals of Arthur's environment in his time, and he was surprisingly knowledgeable. Arthur was intrigued by Iolani's understanding of microorganisms. He'd been entirely ignorant of their existence. If he was off duty Abacha would be with them, probably enticing them to play him at xiangqi.

Wright watched his interface.

The volume in the room decreased as Carol slowly restored order. The mood had turned convivial. Perhaps the meeting wasn't as ridiculous as it had seemed. Maintaining good morale was important to the success of the mission.

With so many disparate individuals aboard along with the pressure of the circumstances and purpose, tension would be high and challenging situations could quickly ignite anger and conflict.

No one knew what lay in wait beyond the Sun's protective cloak. Merlin, Morgan, or another of their species could envelope the *Dauntless* as a black cloud and transport her millions of kilometers, scrambling the brains of everyone aboard. Anything could happen. Literally anything. What the interfering aliens had done defied humanity's understanding of the universe.

Wright thought of Taylan.

He closed his eyes.

When he opened them again, he found himself looking at the screen in the palm of his hand.

Carol was saying something about an obstacle course initiates must complete in their underwear.

"Sir," Wright said, "if I might interrupt?"

"Oh, *now* you're interested," Carol joked. "You don't want to be seen in your briefs. Is that it?"

The room filled with laughter. Even Colbourn smiled.

"No, sir, it's just—"

"You're worried about younger men completing the course faster than you? I thought you got your dicky knee fixed."

Wright clenched his jaw. "Sir, could I speak?"

"Of course, Major. Go ahead." Carol turned to Colbourn as if to whisper something in her ear and ignore whatever Wright had to say.

"We've already passed through the heliopause."

Carol turned back. "What?"

"While everyone was talking, we crossed the heliopause."

"But that isn't possible!"

"The FTL drive is working better than expected. The predicted time for entering interstellar space has been moving forward for the last few hours. I'm sorry, sir. I thought you knew."

"Well, I..." Carol spluttered. "No one told me."

"That's it?" asked the American. "We're already here? No ceremony, nothing?"

An awkward pause followed.

27

———

On Earth, the passing of the *Dauntless* into interstellar space was widely celebrated. The people aboard her were able to view the parties, current affairs programs, and other commemorative events via comm. On the ship, however, the event had been anti-climactic. The attempt to organize shipboard ceremonies had failed in a dismal and embarrassing way, and everyday life had continued as normal.

The *Dauntless's* hull dealt with the increased radiation levels well and nothing else beyond the heliosphere seemed to pose an additional threat to human life. The astrophysicists took their readings and made their observations, but the information wasn't made generally available.

Wright found that, like his time on the *Resolute*, the greatest challenge was to stay occupied and fight off the encroaching boredom of long days with not very much to do. He wasn't high up enough to be responsible for important organizational tasks, nor lowly enough for menial housekeeping duties. Colbourn seemed to think keeping watch on Orr would take up most of his time, but he was lucky to set eyes on her more than once per Active Shift. If she wasn't forced to leave her cabin to eat he doubted he would see her at all.

Orr wasn't who was on his mind most of the time.

Arthur was.

Though the king's mood appeared to have returned to normal after he'd overcome his disappointment about Taylan's decision to remain on Earth, his physical state seemed in decline. Wright had begun to notice the change in Arthur before he performed his disappearing act and caught a train to Cardiff. Gray hairs had appeared in his hair and beard and faint lines were traced on his face. Before, the king had looked ageless. Now, he definitely didn't look his real age of several thousand years, but Wright would have put him at late thirties or early forties.

And as the days passed, Arthur continued to visibly age.

Wright guessed he must have been in his early thirties when Merlin had somehow frozen his natural physical decline ad mummified him in the mountain cave. People grew up young then and were lucky to make it to old age. Yet he hadn't continued to age normally when he was brought back to life. He was growing old faster, as if catching up for lost time.

Wright hadn't talked to him about it. There didn't seem to be much point, and who liked being told they were getting older? As far as he knew, no one else mentioned it to Arthur either. Perhaps no one else had noticed.

Then something else about Arthur changed.

He arrived to eat dinner with Wright, Abacha, and Iolani in the mess. As he walked up to the table, Wright vaguely noticed he looked different. When he studied Arthur more closely, he realized the king was chalk white. He watched him sit down and saw the man's hands tremble.

Iolani had noticed his odd demeanor too. "Is everything

okay?" she asked, pouring him a beaker of water. "You look like you saw a ghost."

At the mention of the word 'ghost' Arthur started and looked around. He grabbed the beaker and gulped the contents. When he put the vessel down he stared at it, his eyes unfocused.

"Arthur?" Abacha gently nudged him.

At his touch the king started again, looked up and saw all three of his companions gazing at him. He attempted a smile though it was more of a grimace. "Nothing's wrong. Please don't be concerned."

Something clearly *was* wrong. Very wrong. But he wasn't about to tell them what it was.

"What do you want to eat?" Wright asked, thinking a change of subject was in order. "The fish curry's good."

"Yes, whatever you recommend." He passed a hand over his forehead and glanced around the mess once more.

Wright walked up to the counter to get Arthur his meal.

When he returned to the table, the king had regained his composure. He wasn't joining in with Iolani and Abacha's conversation, but the color had returned to his face and he appeared calmer.

"Have you seen Kala Orr lately?" Abacha asked as Wright sat down.

"Not today," he replied, putting down a plate in front of Arthur. "I saw her telling off the cook yesterday for not providing eggs at breakfast."

Iolani chuckled. "No chickens aboard a military starship? Who would have thought?"

"God knows what she used to expect from her crews," said Wright. "I hate to think. Probably asses' milk for her baths and fried larks' tongues for snacks."

"Aren't you supposed to be looking after her?" asked Abacha.

"Looking after her? More like stopping her from killing anyone. Have you forgotten about Boots on the *Resolute*?"

Iolani frowned. "Boots? What's wrong with her wearing boots?"

"Boots is the name of Taylan's cat," Abacha explained. "I never met a less house-trained moggie."

"Don't be too hard on him," said Wright. "At least, not if Taylan's around, if you know what's good for you. He got better anyway. I'd say a nine out of ten success rate at hitting the kitty litter."

"What did Orr do to the cat?" asked Iolani.

"Tried to kill him, of course," Wright replied.

She chuckled again. "I like the way you say 'of course' like it was a natural conclusion."

"Isn't it? What else does she do except complain and spread death and destruction wherever she goes? The woman's a walking, talking blight on living things."

"I wonder what made her like that?" asked Abacha.

"Does anything have to have made her like that?" Wright countered. "Isn't it possible she was just born that way?"

"I heard she grew up on the streets in Berline," said Abacha.

"And?" asked Wright. "She wouldn't have been the only one. Did they all turn into megalomaniacal psychopaths? No," he added without waiting for Abacha's reply, "they didn't."

While they'd been talking, Arthur had been mechanically eating his dinner. He put down his fork and said, "You're forgetting Morgan's influence on her. If you must place blame for someone's actions, TJ, place it on the true originator of the evil —Morgan le Fay."

Wright snorted with incredulity. "Come on. Are you saying Orr had no free will? She *chose* to listen to Morgan because it suited her. They both wanted the same things. Orr was the one who freed Morgan from captivity too, don't forget. Why would she free someone who was controlling her?"

"It was probably a mistake," said Arthur. "Morgan would have tricked her."

"Why is everyone so full of excuses for Kala Orr all of a sudden?" asked Wright. "First Abacha's blaming her genocidal behavior on poverty and deprivation, and now you're telling me everything she did was Morgan's fault."

"Not entirely," said Arthur.

"No," said Abacha. "I'm just saying things aren't black and white. Human beings are complicated."

"Never a truer word spoken," said Iolani. "Give me microbes any day. Nice and easy to understand—usually. Would anyone like dessert?"

She began to stand up but before she was upright, an alarm blasted out. She winced and raised her shoulders. "What's that?" she shouted over the noise.

At the same time, Wright received a comm via his implant. "Security breach."

He ran from the mess.

NATURALLY, Orr was behind it. And, also naturally, Colbourn had reached her before Wright and was ready and waiting with an accusatory stare by the time he arrived.

Orr was under restraint in the passageway outside of the FTL drive control room. He learned she'd been inside the room, though no one seemed to know how she got in. There were no guards posted, but a high-level security panel prevented unauthorized entry. No one had seen any need for greater security. Why would anyone want to tamper with the operation of the drive? It could be insanely dangerous for everyone aboard, including the person doing the tampering.

They'd underestimated Orr and the suicidal tendencies of her cult.

Two operators had been present in the room with her. If it hadn't been for the arrival of a third operator as the shift switched, Orr might have succeeded in whatever she was there to do. At the sight of the former Dwyr, the third operator had immediately raised the alarm without waiting for an explanation from his colleagues. There *could* be no rational explanation for her presence near the sensitive, vital equipment except that she meant to do harm.

The third operator had wrestled her outside and restrained her until Wright's arrival. He took over from the man and listened to his story. Orr was limp and unresistant. Colbourn was furious, judging by the set of her jaw.

"When support arrives," she snapped, "I want you to return her to her cabin and set an armed guard. She'll stay there until a decision is made regarding her long-term status on the ship. My recommendation will be she is confined in the brig for the duration of the voyage."

"Yes, ma'am."

The daggers from Colbourn's eyes accused him of failing in his duty but she didn't verbalize her reprimand, no doubt due to the presence of others.

"See me in my office as soon as you're free," said the brigadier.

That would be when he would have strips torn off him.

Two Marines appeared at the end of the passageway. Wright pushed Orr toward them, and they set off.

"You're going to space me, aren't you?" Orr asked.

"What? No. Did you hear what Brigadier Colbourn said? I'm taking you to your cabin."

"You said you would space me if I stepped out of line."

One of the Marines glanced at him.

"I'm going to do exactly as ordered," Wright retorted.

"You'll wait for a chance to get me to an airlock," said Orr. "You'll bribe the guards to turn a blind eye, and that'll be it."

"You're talking nonsense."

"But I won't die," Orr went on.

There was a new tone in her voice that caused Wright to stare at her. It was a note of sadness and self-pity he'd never heard from her before, not in the many days of her obnoxious presence in his life. The tone evoked a twinge of sympathy.

Dammit.

He'd been listening to Abacha and Arthur too much. They didn't understand what a truly despicable person she was.

He didn't want to even speak to her, but curiosity overcame his resolve. "What do you mean you won't die?"

"Only Arthur can kill me."

"Oh, believe me, space will kill you. Not," he added, mindful of the two Marines, "that I plan on putting you out of the ship."

"No, it won't. Nothing will. That's what Morgan told me. She said I am inviolable, and I believe her. Except against Arthur. Merlin gave him special powers to break through my defense."

"I don't know what you're talking about," Wright replied. In fact, he did. Arthur wasn't affected by pulse rounds. It was possible Morgan had done something similar to Orr, though whether the aliens' protections were effective now they were gone was another matter.

"It will be like when Morgan trapped me in my mind," Orr went on. "I will float in space, unable to hear or touch anything, unable to do anything. Except this time I'll see. I'll see the stars. I won't be able to bring my life to an end. I'll be forced to live like that until I die of old age, alone and insane."

The melancholy underlying her words set Wright's nerves on edge.

"Please don't space me," she asked him. "Ask Arthur to kill me—with his sword. That will do it. Only give me time to write to Perran first. And deliver the letter when you get back. I don't think that's too much to ask."

They'd arrived at her cabin at last. Wright thumbed the door release and told the guards to put her inside.

She turned and caught him with a desolate glare.

He shivered, unable to look away until the closing door severed their gazes.

28

———

Orr had been taken from her cabin and confined to the brig. Weeks had passed, and Wright's only occupation now was to ensure the Marines under his command fulfilled their duties. They were exemplary men and women—otherwise they wouldn't have been picked for the mission—so he had very little to do. He found himself spending more and more time with Iolani. She was similarly bored. Her role was to advise on extra-terrestrial life forms they encountered, and there was no chance of that happening at least until they explored the destined planet, perhaps never.

He would often meet her in the briefing room, which doubled as an entertainment lounge for non-military and off-duty military personnel. But they would only go there if the place was comparatively empty, when no vids or holos were playing and no one had organized a game night or other distraction. Otherwise they would go to the mess between meal times. He craved peace and quiet and Iolani seemed to feel the same.

He liked to listen to her talk about her work and Suriname, the country where she'd lived for many years before Ua Talman hired her as a consultant. In turn, she would ask him about life as a Marine. He only told her funny stories, like the sweepstake Lieutenant Ford had run on the *Resolute*, betting on how many words Krol would say at one time before they reached the BI. There was no benefit to either of them in telling her what being in the military was really like. She didn't need to hear about the re-taking of Jamaica or his nightmares and flashbacks.

One day, when they were in the lounge, she asked him about Arthur. Only two other groups of people were in there: the man from the States who had been at the ridiculous Crossing the Line ceremony meeting was with Major-General Bobbin and another North American, and four off-duty ship's technicians sat together drinking beer.

"Is it really true Arthur was dead when you found him?" Iolani suddenly asked.

They'd been talking about the king's apparent physical decline. Iolani had noticed it too, but, like Wright, she didn't know what to do about her observation.

"Is that the rumor?" Wright asked. "No, he wasn't dead. He only looked dead. My HUD told me he was alive, though just barely."

"Your HUD?"

"Heads-Up Display on my helmet visor."

"Ah, I see. Your suit scanned him?"

"Exactly. We can scan for vital signs." He didn't elaborate.

"It's astounding, isn't it?"

"That he stayed alive so long? I didn't believe it myself for a long time, even though I was there as he recovered. He looked like a mummy at first but within days he'd transformed to a normal, healthy adult man. It was only when Merlin turned up that things began to make sense. I think it's clear the alien did something to Arthur to keep him alive."

"There are creatures on Earth that have survived longer than Arthur," said Iolani. "Organisms that were frozen for tens of thousands of years then revived. So it's possible, though I can't imagine how it would work for human beings."

"Arthur wasn't frozen, only dried up. It was cold in the cave but not below freezing."

"Scientists have managed to sprout seeds that are thousands of years old. I wish I'd been there when Arthur was found. I could have learned so much. It's a shame the doctors on your ship didn't contact someone qualified to study what was happening."

"It was all top secret at the time," said Wright. "The medics probably kept records and you could apply to read them, but, to be honest, it's unlikely you would get permission."

"That's what I thought." Iolani chewed her lip.

Wright was quiet too.

On the other side of the room, one of the Americans guffawed.

Iolani looked up and held his gaze without speaking. Suddenly the atmosphere between them shifted. He began to feel uncomfortable.

Shit.

He'd been hanging out with Hale almost daily for a long time. Sometimes Arthur or Abacha was with them, sometimes both of them were, but the constant had been he and Iolani. Had he been leading her on? He didn't think so, but he couldn't be sure. Yet they were both single and she was an attractive woman who, as far as he knew, wasn't close to anyone else on the ship.

"TJ, I..." Her voice petered out. Perhaps she'd read the panic on his face.

He should set her straight, but how to do it? He was terrible at anything like this, entirely out of practice. He rubbed the top of his head. "Iolani—"

A dreadful moaning came from the passageway. The lounge

door was closed, but the sound penetrated the room, silencing everyone.

Wright stared at the doorway. "What the...?"

The sound was almost inhuman, though no other living things were aboard. Had Orr escaped from the brig? The noise was deep-pitched, but her voice was low for a woman.

Whoever it was, she or he sounded utterly terrified.

The door slid open, activated automatically by movement outside. Arthur stumbled in backwards. It was he who was making the ghastly noise. His arms flailing, he fell to the floor. He turned onto his front and began to crawl from the open doorway, his features fixed by abject horror.

Arthur was not easily scared. Wright had seen him fight. What was the cause of his dismay?

A giant whooping gasp came from his left, and Iolani's fingers dug into his arm.

Then he saw it too.

A figure was floating into the room. Wispy, almost transparent, and entirely white, it was the image of a tall, slim woman. She was dressed in the style of Arthur's time, a long robe falling to her feet pulled in at her waist by a slim belt. Her hair hung down her back from her high forehead. Her near-invisibility made it hard to see the detail of her face but she seemed beautiful.

Arthur had crawled as far as he could go. He sat on the deck, his back against the bulkhead, his forearms crossed protectively over his eyes and his head averted. "Begone! Begone, phantom. Bother me no more."

"Holy shit," whispered Major-General Bobbin.

Wright then heard her mumble as she spoke into her comm and he realized with a start he should be doing the same.

But what should he say? *Major Wright to Control. Ghost in the briefing room. I repeat, ghost in the briefing room.*

Arthur's tormentor was hanging over him, the king clearly

visible through her gown. She seemed to be trying to speak to him. Her hands gestured smoothly and gently as if she was explaining something.

"No!" Arthur exclaimed. "No, I will not heed you. You are dead. You are long dead." He continued to speak but not in English. He'd switched to his original language.

There was a sudden movement as the four techies sprang for the door. Wright remembered Iolani was a civilian. "Get behind me," he told her, placing a hand on his sidearm.

"I don't think it's dangerous," she said. "It seems to want to communicate."

He moved in front of her anyway.

But the thing was already fading. It continued to move its arms and hands, but it was growing rapidly fainter.

Within seconds it had vanished.

Wright crossed the room to Arthur, who was a trembling wreck.

"It's gone," he reassured him. "Whatever the hell that thing was, it's gone. You don't have to be afraid."

The king's eyes remained wild with fear and his breathing was ragged.

"Should I call a medic?" Wright asked.

"No." Arthur swallowed. "No. I'm not unwell." He breathed more deeply and his facial muscles lost some of their rigidity. He was staring at the door, seeming to expect the 'ghost' to return any minute. He switched focus to Wright. "You saw it too?"

Iolani had joined them. "We all did."

Tension melted from Arthur. "I thought I was going mad. I thought I was imagining her."

"You've seen it before?" Wright asked. Then he recalled the time in the mess when Arthur had appeared to have received a shock of some kind.

"I have seen her several times. Usually, I would run away.

That was the first time she followed me. I thought she would never leave me."

Iolani asked, "Do you know who it was?"

"I know who it looks like. It resembles my queen, every detail perfect, exactly as I remember her. But it is not her. Not unless Merlin preserved her too, and I'm sure he didn't. He never liked Guinevere. No, if you can see it too it is a phantasm, perhaps created by Morgan le Fay. It was sent here to strike fear into my heart. I thought she only appeared in my imagination, not in reality."

"She's as real as ghosts get," said a voice. The American who had been at the meeting was peering at Arthur.

Two armed Marines burst in. Bobbin's comm had drawn a response.

"The crisis is over," Wright told them. "You can return to duty."

Arthur sank his face into his hands. "What am I to do, TJ? What am I to do?"

29

Wright moved into Arthur's cabin. It was a squeeze. There was no room for another bunk so he had to sleep on a mattress on the deck. The king had wanted to swap places with him, but Wright insisted on taking the less comfortable option. It was no great inconvenience, especially not compared to fielding the vision of Guinevere that kept appearing.

She didn't turn up frequently, but when she did it always seemed to be when least expected. One time, late in the Quiet Shift, Wright had woken to see the figure, faintly luminescent, hovering directly above him. She'd seemed to want Arthur as she always did, but luckily he'd remained sound asleep.

Another time she appeared to Arthur while he was in the shower. He came barreling out into the main cabin yelling his head off, stark naked and soaking wet. That time, she only stuck around a couple of minutes before disappearing.

There was nothing Wright could do to protect him. The phenomenon occurred randomly with no warning or precursors, and nothing affected it. It couldn't be touched and pulse rounds passed through it. None of the scientists aboard could even hazard a guess about what the specter was. They had rigged up Arthur's cabin with cameras and sensors, but all the information they'd gleaned was a slight increase in the atmospheric electrical charge whenever the apparition appeared. No black clouds in the surrounding space accompanied it, so Arthur's theory it was something to do with the aliens Morgan or Merlin remained unsupported.

Despite the repetition of the visits, Arthur's terror didn't abate. Each time he encountered the thing, he acted as shocked and horrified as he'd been in the briefing room. Whereas Wright had found the 'ghost' disturbing at first, but he grew more curious about the figure than frightened by it. He guessed the king's reaction had something to do with his religious background. He had a deep-seated fear of anything that seemed evil or demonic, and there was also the fact that the apparition looked like his dead wife.

So the days passed, Wright keeping Arthur company while waiting for another visit from Guinevere's ghost. He'd tried to engage the king in conversation about the queen once or twice, but he'd quickly given up after it became clear how painful the subject was to him. Wright knew too well how hard affairs of the heart were to put into words. He hadn't managed to speak to Iolani about her take on their friendship, which he suspected she felt was something more. Perhaps it was for the best.

Between Arthur and the life scientist, he'd almost forgotten about Kala Orr. It had been a relief to put her out of his mind when she'd been confined to the brig.

So it was a surprise and a harsh return to reality when Colbourn's sharp command arrived in his head. "Major, attend Orr in the brig immediately. She's kicking off about something and the guards can't get her under control."

"Yes, Brigadier." He excused himself to Arthur and sped from the cabin.

The brig was a two-minute jog away. When Wright arrived,

Orr was covered in blood and wrestling with two guards in her cell. The place was awash with blood too, and the three were slipping and sliding on it as they fought.

"She tried to top herself," one of the guards explained.

"Are medics on their way?" he asked. Colbourn must have misunderstood the nature of the emergency.

"Yeah, we called them first," said the other guard. "You must have been nearer."

Before she'd finished her sentence, a medical team ran in. Wright stepped up to Orr, who was struggling with a wild frenzy. One guard was attempting to get her arm behind her back, but it was slick with blood and Orr seemed to have the strength of a couple of men. The other guard was on her knees, holding Orr's thighs in a bear grip.

"Get her on the deck," Wright snapped. He grappled the former Dwyr around her hips and lifted her struggling body off her feet.

She lashed out with both legs and he fought to maintain his grip on her torso. Her clothes were soaked in blood. There was so much of it, it was hard to tell where it was coming from.

Hadn't she said she couldn't die? That only Arthur could put an end to her life? If she really thought that, what was the point of what she'd been attempting?

The guard at her back forced her forward and the three of them managed to lay her on her front.

"Turn her over," said a medic.

Orr's utterances had been mostly incoherent until now. As Wright rolled her, she screamed, "Don't touch me! How dare you touch me! Get your hands off me you disgusting wretches." She worked her mouth as if preparing to spit. Wright clamped a hand over it to prevent her but also to shut her up.

"Does anyone know where she's cut?" the medic asked.

"Wrists, I think," said a guard.

The other medic arrived with a pressure hypodermic and

thrust it into her bicep, depressing the button. Orr's eyes rolled back and her body went limp.

"Phew!" a guard exclaimed, releasing her hold. "Thank fuck for that." She stiffened and glanced at Wright. "Sorry, sir."

"Never mind." He stood up. Smears of Orr's blood covered his uniform.

The medics moved in, turning over her arms to examine her wrists. Deep gashes marked them. A meter or so away, a jagged piece of plastic lay on the deck, one edge wet and red. It looked like it had been broken from a food tray.

"What happened?" he asked.

The guard who had sworn replied, "I gave her her food about half an hour ago. When I checked to see if she'd finished, I saw her on her bunk and a pool of blood on the floor. I raised the alarm and asked Jarvis here for assistance. We went in to try to stop the bleeding until medical could get here but, well, you saw how she reacted, sir."

"Yeah," the other guard remarked. "She was serious, not attention-seeking."

"She certainly was," a medic commented. "She went down to the bone on this arm."

Colbourn comm'd him. "SITREP, Major."

"The situation's under control, ma'am. It was a medical emergency. Attempted suicide."

"Attempted? So she's still alive?"

"For now, ma'am. I expect you'll receive a report soon."

"Good. Wouldn't want her dying on us while she might still be useful."

The coldness of Colbourn's words hit him. *While she might still be useful?*

Wright looked down on Orr, unconscious and pale where she wasn't bloody. She'd lost considerable weight since the last time he'd seen her weeks ago. What had driven her to try to take her own life? After her attempt to sabotage the FTL drive, she'd been scared he would space her. But he hadn't. He'd left her alone in the brig. She had to know by now she was safe from him. So what else was bothering her? Was she missing her position as Dwyr? Was life meaningless to her if she wasn't adored and worshipped by millions? Or was she missing her son?

"She's stable," said a medic. "Let's get her on the gurney."

"She put up a heck of a fight considering the state she's in," the other remarked as they lifted her. "She's lucky to be alive. Look at the blood. Gotta be a couple of liters here."

The other nodded. "At least. Come on, let's get her to the bay."

A gasp from one of the guards made them pause.

Then Wright saw it too.

An apparition, like the one Arthur had been seeing, had appeared near Orr's bunk.

Except it was not exactly like Arthur's. It was white, faintly luminous, and nearly transparent, but it didn't look like Guinevere. This image was of a small man, bent with age. A straggly beard adorned his face and long, thin, unkempt hair hung to his shoulders. He wore a knee-length nightshirt and a single fluffy slipper. The figure floated toward where Orr lay on the gurney.

"Shoot it!" yelled a medic, dragging the gurney toward the door.

"No point," said Wright.

The specter of the man halted and hovered over Orr. The translucent lines of its lips moved but no sound came out. All that could be heard was the labored breathing of the spectacle's witnesses.

The medics hastily departed with Orr.

The apparition didn't follow.

"What should we do, sir?" asked a guard.

"Nothing. It should disappear soon."

Even as he spoke the edges of the old man were becoming less distinct.

"I heard about what happened in the briefing room," said the guard. "Never thought I'd see it myself. What's it doing here, I wonder?"

Wright was wondering if it had something to do with Orr's attempted suicide. Arthur had certainly been driven to distraction by the phenomenon. It seemed significant that he and Orr, both of whom had been close to Merlin and Morgan respectively, should be the targets of these visits.

30

———

"You're to accompany Dwyr Orr for her psychiatric evaluation," Colbourn told Wright. She'd called him into her office to discuss the Marines' ongoing strategy regarding Orr.

He felt like asking, *Why me?*

"Yes, Brigadier."

"She's extremely unstable according to her medical report, but Dr Kim won't allow anyone except the patient in her office during treatment sessions, unfortunately. I explained the risks but she isn't having it, and sadly we don't have any facilities that would give the doctor the necessary protection. No one imagined our resident psychiatrist would be dealing with dangerous patients."

Orr had been put on suicide watch and would be returning to the brig today. Her cell had been fitted with the same equipment as Arthur's cabin in case Orr's apparition returned.

"So I'll wait outside?" he asked.

"Exactly."

Why she wanted *him* at Orr's psychiatric assessment, he couldn't understand. A couple of tough, armed guards would do. But the brigadier had associated him with Orr ever since he'd brought the woman to the BI on the *Resolute*. Maybe that was it. Or maybe Colbourn thought he might be useful in a psychiatric crisis due to his own problems.

"Yes, ma'am."

"Now."

"I'm sorry?"

"She's being escorted to see Kim now."

"Oh, I see."

Colbourn bent her head to scan her interface, dismissing him with her body language.

He left and headed for Dr Kim's office. The psychiatrist was alone. He'd arrived before Orr.

"Hello, Major. Please, sit down."

"But…"

"We have a few minutes. I'd like to talk to you. See how things are going."

Colbourn's intention became clear. She'd hoodwinked him.

Resigned, he lowered himself into the empty seat. Kim sat across from him. The doctor was gangly, dressed in civilian clothes, her short black hair peppered gray. She crossed one leg over the other at the knee.

"We don't have long," she said, "so I'll come straight to the point. I'm surprised and a little concerned that you haven't been to see me yet."

He sighed. "Given my history, you mean?"

She nodded.

"I haven't felt any need."

"You were advised to attend regular psychiatric evaluations. It isn't a punishment, you know. This is for your own well-being and that of those under your command."

He stiffened. "No one in my command has ever been in any danger from me."

"You misunderstand. To exercise sound judgment an officer must be of sound mind."

"I *am* of sound mind."

She fixed him with her gaze. "In your opinion, I'm sure you are. Most people feel the same, regardless of their mental status. How have you been sleeping lately?"

"Well enough."

"Still getting flashbacks?"

He let out a long breath. "Occasionally, but I can deal with them."

"Thank you for being honest. That's a good sign. The methods you were taught at the clinic are working for you?"

"Yes."

Mostly.

"Good. You remember how to self-assess to tell if things are getting bad again?"

"*Yes.*"

She smiled tightly. "Right, that's it. I only wanted to touch base with you and remind you I'm here if you need me. Your responsibilities with Kala Orr and now Arthur have put you under a lot of pressure. It can't be easy for you."

She got to her feet and walked to the door. When it slid open she looked out. "No sign of her. We still have a little time." Sitting down again, she continued, "To be honest, Major, I asked Colbourn to send you here early so I could squeeze in a quick consult. I am absolutely snowed under and I didn't want to ask you to wait for an appointment if you needed one."

"You've had lots of requests for treatment?"

"Yes, and plenty of treatment orders. As I was saying, many don't realize they may have a problem."

He was puzzled. The *Dauntless's* crew were the best the Alliance had to offer, and the passengers would have been psychologically vetted before they were allowed aboard.

"I know what you're thinking," said Kim. "How come I'm in

so much demand? I've wondered about that as well. I expected to be bored on this long voyage with few people who might need my help. But the opposite is the case. I'm rushed off my feet. My waiting list is a week long."

"What sort of problems are you seeing, if you don't mind me asking?"

"Depression, apathy, interpersonal tension, lack of affect, anxiety... I don't have anything concrete yet, but—"

The door to her office opened. Orr stood between two guards, or, rather, she sagged and they held her upright by her arms. She looked ghastly. The apparition that had appeared in her cell had looked healthier. Her wrists were bound with dressings.

Wright vacated his seat as the guards brought Orr over. "I'll wait outside."

Dr Kim spent longer than an hour with her, despite her assertion that she was busy. Her next appointment, a young officer cadet arrived. She flushed when she saw Wright and the two guards and retreated several meters down the passageway.

As Wright kicked his heels, he mulled over the odd phenomena of the two apparitions, one striking terror into its subject, the other driving its target to suicidal despair. The *Dauntless* was months into her long journey but she had months of FTL travel ahead of her too. What kind of state would Arthur and Orr be in by the time they arrived if the ethereal visits continued?

He was well past bored of waiting when Kim's office door eventually opened and Orr appeared. She didn't look a whole lot better than she had when she'd gone in. Maybe she seemed a tad less melancholy.

He walked with her and the guards to the brig. When they reached it, he stepped into her cell and asked the guards to wait outside.

She flopped onto her bunk and curled up into a fetal position, her back toward him.

"Kala, I—"

"How dare you," she murmured. "You shall address me as…" She exhaled, long and soft.

"I want to ask you about the thing that appeared after you cut your wrists."

Silence.

"I'm guessing it wasn't the first time it's been here. Was that why you wanted to die? Because you couldn't stand it anymore?"

Nothing.

He waited, hoping she might say something, even if it was only to tell him to leave her alone.

"Are you aware something has been visiting Arthur too?" he asked eventually. "We've been wondering if it's something to do with Morgan, or perhaps Merlin. Do you think she could be sending these things into the ship in order to terrorize both of you?"

Orr remained quiet and still, her chest barely moving with her respirations. She wasn't asleep. He was sure of it. He needed her to talk. They needed all the information they could get on these strange beings repeatedly appearing within the ship. If Orr knew or just guessed something, he needed to know.

"The one that visits Arthur is always in the shape of his former queen," he said. "Is your visitor always the same? Do you recognize it? Is the old man someone you know or used to know?"

After several seconds, an almost-inaudible, "Yes."

He perked up. "You know him?"

Orr didn't answer. Perhaps that was all he was going to get.

"Is the man still alive?" he asked. It probably wasn't important, but he wanted to get her talking again. "Or is he dead, like Guinevere?"

Her chest expanded as she took a deep breath. She turned onto her back and stared at the overhead as she answered, "Dead."

"What was your relationship with him?"

Tears slid from her eyes to her pillow. "He was a friend. An old friend."

A *friend*? He couldn't imagine her having friends. Sycophants, yes. Hangers on, sure. People too scared of her to tell her what they really thought of her, of course. But a genuine friend? She had to be mistaken.

"Do you know what's behind these visits? Did Morgan ever create something like that?"

She swallowed. "I don't know what's behind them. Morgan could be doing it. I don't know why she would, but she's capable of many things."

"Is there anything you can tell me that might help us understand what's happening?"

He waited, but she only continued to stare into the middle distance, not speaking.

Did she know something but was refusing to answer or was she really as ignorant as everyone else aboard? If she really wanted to die, maybe she simply didn't care what happened. And she was Kala Orr, who famously didn't give a shit about others anyway.

He watched her, but then he turned his attention to the small cell. The blood from her suicide attempt had been cleaned away and the sanobots must have removed any specks the cleaners had missed. The place was bare, sterile, and nearly empty.

How many meters stood between Orr and he and the hull? Ten or twelve, he guessed. And then beyond the hull was the vastness of interstellar space. They were already light years from Earth, wrapped in the warp bubble that allowed them to slip through the black at unimaginable speed. They had light years to travel before they would arrive at their destination, a place inhabited by nothing more than microbes at best and which was hostile to human life.

Two hundred souls, ensconced in a vessel not even as large as a speck on the cosmic scale. Tiny, unimportant living beings, whose life spans were perhaps no more than seconds compared to their alien tormentors', according to Iolani. If the FTL drive were to explode and wipe them all out in an instant, the event would be utterly inconsequential in galactic terms.

They were meaningless and alone in the expanse.

Orr was looking at him.

Across the boundless distance between their backgrounds, beliefs, desires, and motivations, his hatred for odious, abhorrent human being eased a notch.

31

W right was walking through the streets of downtown Jamaica. His platoon had escaped the barricade set by the EAC forces with the help of the Jamaican Resistance, and they were on their way to the field hospital set up at the ambassador's residence.

As he walked, he scanned carefully for hostiles. Crusaders were notoriously suicidal and would take ridiculous risks to attack the Alliance. They were all over the city too, small cells remaining in many places, refusing to surrender.

He spotted a familiar figure ahead.

Sometimes, identifying his men and women by sight wasn't easy. Their armor and tinted visors made them anonymous. But this figure was smaller than most and bore the stripe of her rank on her shoulder. He switched his HUD to show each Marines' name to check.

It was her!

He was confused. Something wasn't right, but he wasn't sure what. Why was he surprised to see her here?

He ran forward.

Patel was walking between two comrades, her rifle across

her chest. The three Marines seemed to be talking on a private comm channel, probably kidding around or gossiping. He tried to comm her directly but she didn't answer.

He grabbed her shoulder. He needed to check it was Patel and figure out what she was doing here when...

Her visor was up.

Her face was gone.

Where there should have been eyes, a nose, a mouth and chin, cheekbones, skin, was a charred, gaping hole.

He screamed.

"*TJ!*"

Hands were on him, shaking him.

He opened his eyes on darkness.

"Sorry," he mumbled. "Another nightmare."

"I know," said Arthur. "I know, but...look."

Wright blinked as he tried to focus. The dream was one that had haunted his sleeping hours for months. He didn't know when or if he would ever be rid of it.

He wanted to remember Patel as the smart, eager, loyal, determined young woman she'd been before she died. He wanted to remember her smile and the flash of her eye, not the horror of her corpse as he'd caught her in his arms.

"Look!" Arthur insisted.

Wright became aware of a glow in what should have been the pitch black of the cabin.

He groaned. Guinevere was back again.

But Arthur seemed unusually calm about it. Perhaps he was getting used to the visits.

Wright rubbed his eyes and squinted into the dark.

The figure hung over them, its lines softly glowing.

Except it wasn't Guinevere. It was a man, but not the one who had appeared in Kala Orr's cell. This one was middle-aged and wearing a suit.

A band fastened around Wright's throat. He choked out a gasp. It couldn't be.

Above him floated his father. He hadn't set eyes on him since his eighteenth birthday. He'd never looked at a picture of him or watched him in a family vid. He'd got rid of everything pertaining to his parents the moment they'd dismissed him from their lives. All he had of them were memories from his childhood.

What did it mean?

Was his dad dead?

He looked the same as he had the last time he'd seen him.

Why was the thing appearing to him? Had Morgan or Merlin invaded his mind and stolen the image to create a vision to scare him?

"Light," said Arthur.

The cabin light came on. The apparition faded in competition with the brightness, but it didn't go away. This one wasn't attempting to communicate. Its mouth and hands were still. It only watched him.

Then it was gone.

"I'm sorry," Arthur said. "I'm sorry it's happening to you too."

Wright reached for his shirt and pulled it on. There would be no more sleep for him tonight. "It isn't your fault. I wish I knew what the hell those things are."

"Perhaps they *are* from hell."

"What do you mean?"

Arthur lay down in his bed and put his hands behind his head. "I've been wondering something, TJ. Do you think maybe we're in hell? I used to think hell was beneath the surface of the Earth, somewhere deep below, from where volcanoes spurt their fire. But what if it is here beyond the sky among the stars? What if the priests are wrong and heaven isn't high up but low down or in another place? What if we've left the Kingdom of God behind and we're traveling into a demonic region?"

Wright stared at him. "You certainly know how to put the wind up someone."

"I'm just thinking aloud."

"I'd appreciate it if you would keep those thoughts to yourself. Things are bad enough around here as it is. Morale's low and most of the crew and passengers are jittery and stressed from what I've heard. The last thing we need is someone putting the idea they might be in hell into their heads. Stars!"

He pushed down his blankets and stood up before pulling on his pants. His hands trembled. He was already shaken up by his nightmare and his father's apparition, let alone Arthur's belief they were in some kind of medieval underworld.

"Major Wright!"

He grimaced.

One day, he would resign from the Royal Marines, get his damned implant removed, and his head would be his own again.

"Yes, Brigadier?"

"Glad you're awake. There's a disturbance in the briefing room. You're the nearest officer. Get over there immediately and make sure you're armed. Shots have been fired. I'm on my way."

"Yes, ma'am."

He quickly put on his boots and, telling Arthur not to leave his cabin, ran into the passageway.

ALL SEEMED quiet in the briefing room, though for some reason the door stood open. Light shone into the passageway. Wright estimated it was about 0300 hours. The room should have been empty. No entertainments would be scheduled at this late hour and most passengers would be asleep. Any crew who were awake would be on duty.

He crept closer, his beamer at the ready.

He halted.

Lying on the deck just inside the doorway was a man on his back, arms splayed out. He wasn't military. He couldn't see any movement of his chest. That was all Wright could tell. One of his knees was bent and lying in the doorway, which explained why the door was open. The sensors were picking up the object in close proximity.

Murmuring just above a whisper, he requested medical support. It was probably already on the way but it wouldn't hurt to make sure.

"Who's out there?" barked a voice. "It took you long enough. Who is it?"

Wright recognized the voice but he couldn't put a name to it. The speaker was male and his accent was upper class, clipped and confident.

The answer came.

"Larson?" he asked. "Is that you?"

"Huh! Well done, Major Wright. You've got it in one. Show your face so I can see you. It isn't polite to shout around corners."

It was RAF Group Captain Larson, who had argued so vehemently at the Crossing the Line meeting.

"What are you doing, Larson?" Wright asked. "Who's that lying in the doorway?"

"Guess."

He heard movement behind him. Colbourn had appeared at the end of the passageway. Two medics crowded behind her. He motioned with his hand for all of them to stay back.

"SITREP, Major," came Colbourn's request over his comm.

He replied very softly, "One civilian is down. Group Captain Larson seems to be responsible. Still assessing the situation."

"A section is on its way," she replied, "approaching from starboard. I'll tell them to halt once they see you and await further orders. Iolani Hale is in there too. I don't know who else."

"Hale?"

"She was the one who got a comm out to the bridge. That's all I know."

"I'm still waiting, Wright," Larson said. "Don't tell me you don't know who it is I helpfully eradicated from the manifest."

"You killed someone?"

"No. I killed some*thing*. There are things living among us and they must be eradicated. They're the ones responsible for the strange appearances. I haven't figured out what they're doing yet or why, but I will get to the bottom of it."

"What are you talking about?" Wright asked. "I don't understand."

"If you don't understand, maybe you're part of the problem."

He had a sudden brainwave. "Brigadier," he comm'd, "I need a helmet."

"Copy. And Dr Kim is on her way."

It was a smart call from Colbourn. Larson did appear to be having some kind of psychotic break.

The section of five Marines appeared at the other end of the passageway and quickly stopped as they saw Wright. They were suited up and armed.

"I want to speak to Iolani," he said.

"You want to speak to Ms Hale? Hm. I'm not sure why. Are you two colluding in the subterfuge? I was so sure it was only the civilian passengers. Perhaps I was wrong."

"Larson, you've already killed an innocent person. Don't make things worse for yourself. Let Iolani go, and anyone else you have in there with you. Give yourself up and we can get you some help."

"I don't need anyone's help!" spat Larson. "I'm doing you all a favor. Why can't you see that? I'm helping you by identifying the aliens and eradicating them."

"How can you be so sure? How do you know you haven't killed an innocent man?"

"I worked it out by logical deduction. Every military person on this ship is Alliance. We've pledged our loyalty and would never do anything to harm the mission. The only people remaining who aren't Alliance are the civilian passengers. Something has infiltrated them, taken them over and is working through them, turning them into saboteurs. They're the ones creating the ghosts. They want to destabilize us, make us afraid, make us turn back."

"If you're correct," said Wright, playing for time, "then all you have to do is come out and explain your theory. Let Iolani and whoever else is in there with you go. We can deal with them if they've really been taken over."

Someone gently touched his shoulder and he nearly jumped out of his skin. Colbourn stood behind him, gun in one hand, a helmet in the other.

He took it and put it on. The HUD lit up and he quietly stated his instructions.

"That's the problem," said Larson. "How will you tell? That's what I've been struggling with. I was sure about the American but what about the others? Which ones are compromised and which are normal? It would be safer to kill them all. I'm not sure I can trust you to do that. I admit I'm finding it hard myself."

Wright had accessed the ship's security system. He had a choice of three views of the briefing room, derived from the cameras inside. He relayed the real-time vids to the Marines waiting opposite him.

"Don't do anything hasty," said Wright. "We have time to talk about this."

"Have we? I'm not too sure about that. I'm not a fool, Major. You're hatching something out there as we speak. In fact..." he added.

There was the whisper of pulse fire and the security images on Wright's HUD died.

"Ha!" said Larson. "Wish I'd thought of that before, but better late than never I suppose."

"Group Captain Larson, this is Dr Kim. I don't believe I've had the pleasure of making your acquaintance."

Kim was standing behind Colbourn. Both women were too close. He gestured for them to get back.

"You brought in the shrink!" Larson exclaimed. "Too predictable for words. I'm disappointed."

"Group Captain," Kim called from her more distant spot, "I know you don't want to hurt anyone. Please put down your weapon and come out, and we can talk."

Wright had only seen a glimpse of the setup in the briefing room. It was enough but he had to act fast before anyone changed position. After giving the Marines brief orders, he took off his helmet. It would be better to send in someone in armor first but there would only be time for one good shot and he wanted to be the one to take it.

He held up his hand, his five digits outspread. He closed in his thumb.

Four.

Three.

Two...

The security cameras had revealed a dismal scene. As well as the one dead civilian lying next to the door, the back of his head destroyed, another corpse lay face down on a table. This man had been shot in the back. It looked as though Larson had shot him first and then fired on the second one as he'd tried to bolt from the room.

That must have been when Iolani had managed to get word

out about what was happening.

Four more men and women crouched in a corner. Wright had recognized the other American who had attended the Crossing the Line meeting. He didn't know the others, and his short appraisal of the scene hadn't revealed if they were all civilians.

Perhaps Larson had caught Iolani comming about the situation, for where he faced the door he had her on her knees in front of him, her back toward him, his gun aimed at her head.

There was no question of allowing Larson a chance to give himself up. The risk to Iolani was too great.

One.

Wright stepped through the open doorway, aimed and fired, hitting the Group Captain in the chest at nearly point blank range. He collapsed onto Hale.

The other Marines sprang into the room and ran to the group in the corner, rifles raised, but it appeared Larson had been acting alone. The four were not armed and were plainly terrified. Wright strode to Iolani, who had curled into a ball on the deck, her arms covering her head.

He kicked Larson's weapon away and lifted the man's body off her. She was smeared with his blood. Miraculously, the man was still alive. He groaned faintly and then, blood bubbling in his throat, exhaled and was still.

Iolani was rigid. When Wright touched her, she didn't move.

"It's okay," he said. "It's over now."

"He's dead?" she whispered.

"Yes, he's dead."

She peeked out.

"It's okay," Wright repeated.

He helped her uncurl. She sat up and he held her, patting her back to reassure her she was safe.

"Good work, Major," said Colbourn.

32

Carol and Colbourn sat together at the meeting to discuss the incident. Arthur was on Colbourn's right. Dr Kim had been invited to report on the psychological status of the crew and passengers, and Hale was here to give her opinion on the nature of the specters that kept appearing. The American—Wright had only just learned his name: Josh Grady—hadn't been invited originally but had insisted on attending.

As soon as Wright heard the man's name, he recognized it. Mr Grady was a business magnate who had built his fortune in the solar power industry, supplying energy to most of the States, Canada, Middle and South America.

In an earlier time, Grady might have been as wealthy as Ua Talman. Centuries ago, the States had been one country, the richest economy in the world and its government the most politically powerful. But over time the wealthiest states sought independence, breaking away and weakening the parent. As being united became less and less beneficial to the remaining states, they also seceded. Within two hundred years, what had once been a mighty nation had become fifty distinct countries, loosely connected by history.

Had Josh Grady been able to lobby for the support of a United States government, had he been able to land contracts worth trillions in the early days of his business, *he* could have been building three colony ships and planning a life in the stars.

As it was, he could only use his influence to secure a seat on the first ship to enter interstellar space and investigate life on another planet.

And nearly lose his life when an air force officer went crazy.

Kim was summarizing her report. "In short, I have serious concerns about the psychological well-being of a significant proportion of the crew and passengers. I cannot foresee these problems improving without intense counseling and medication, treatments which, as the only psychiatrist aboard with limited medical supplies, I cannot adequately provide. These problems will only become more exacerbated as our voyage progresses. My recommendation is that the *Dauntless* turns back immediately, or we are likely to see similar incidents to the one in the briefing room, perhaps on a larger scale."

"That decides it," said Grady. "The doctor has spoken. It's time to turn the ship around."

"Mr Grady," said Carol, "I know you aren't a military man, but I shouldn't have to remind you this is a BA endeavor. While we will take Dr Kim's opinion into consideration, the decision to abandon the mission lies with the Alliance and the Alliance only. Thank you, Dr Kim."

He shifted in his seat to address the room.

"Now hold on," Grady protested. "I was nearly killed back there. One of my very good friends was shot in the back by a madman. You aren't seriously suggesting we carry on? I demand that we return to Earth. You can't keep me here against my will. That's kidnapping."

Colbourn fixed him with her trademark icy glare. "You are a *guest* aboard this ship. You have no say in her operation and no sway over Alliance strategy. If you have trouble understanding that, check the contract you signed."

"I'll contact my lawyers," Grady threatened. "I have direct, instant comm to my office, don't forget. You won't hear the last of this."

"She's right," Iolani said wearily. "As civilians, what we want doesn't count. We're entirely in the hands of the Alliance. If it wanted to fly the *Dauntless* into a star there wouldn't be a thing we could do about it, and our relatives would have no come back."

"Thank you for putting it so succinctly," said Carol. "Nevertheless, we are naturally taking the incident in the briefing room very seriously. Clearly the strange phenomena of the spectral appearances is creating an atmosphere of alarm and suspicion."

"Scapegoating is a typical reaction in these circumstances," said Kim. "Larson was looking for someone to blame for his fear and a way to put an end to the perceived threat. If we do continue the mission, we can only expect to see similar events. By the way, I'd like to state for the record I object to the way the situation with Larson was resolved. I should have been allowed the opportunity to talk to him."

Wright said, "He'd killed two people already and he was holding his gun against the head of another. No one regrets Larson's death more than I, but I wasn't going to risk him shooting someone else."

"Absolutely," said Colbourn. "I stand behind Major Wright's actions one hundred percent."

Kim responded, "There should have been a discussion—"

"There was no time!" Wright passed a hand over his eyes. Did she think he *wanted* to kill the man? "He had Iolani at gunpoint and four more unarmed civilians with him."

"Dr Kim," said Carol, "Group Captain Larson knew the risks when he signed up. His death is regrettable but I agree with Brigadier Colbourn and Major Wright—in the circumstances, it was unavoidable. You've stated your opinion. It's time to move on."

"If she's right and we can expect to see more of this," Grady said, "we should turn back!"

Ignoring him, Carol asked Kim, "Do you have any suggestions on what we can do to put minds at ease and reduce the possibility of a recurrence?"

"The best option would be to prevent the figures from reappearing. That would help to reduce the current excessive mental strain."

"Do you think the two phenomena are connected?" he asked "Could these things be infiltrating our brains?"

"I wouldn't jump to that conclusion. I believe what we're seeing among the crew and passengers is a sane reaction to an insane environment. This is the first time human beings have entered interstellar space. Some psychological fall out is only to be expected."

"But every single person aboard had either been thoroughly assessed or has already logged years aboard starships."

"Living within a few days' or weeks' travel of Earth is quite different from leaving the home planet far behind, Lieutenant-General," said Kim. She paused before going on, "Identifying what the things visiting us are might help. Fear of the unknown is what's preying on many minds, in my opinion. Of course, that includes fear of the new territory of deep space, but there isn't much we can do about that."

"Ms Hale," said Carol, turning to her. "You're our resident expert on alien life. Do you have anything to say?"

"I'm *not* an expert on xeno-organisms," she retorted. "It's a new field. There are no experts. I'm sorry, I have no idea what those things are. All I can tell you is they aren't organic. They seem to be pure energy. You might be better off talking to the astrophysicists."

Carol huffed in frustration. "What about you Arthur? You seem to be the one they've visited the most, though we aren't sure about their history with Kala Orr."

The king shook his head. "I thought mine could be a creation of Morgan le Fay's. She knew Guinevere. But if Morgan hadn't conjured her, I thought perhaps she was a demon, come to punish me for my sins. I committed many due to Merlin's false counsel. When I learned Kala Orr was receiving visits from a phantasm too, my thoughts turned to Morgan again. But then Major Wright's father appeared, and now I am simply confused."

"Wright has a spectral visitor?" Carol said. "Why wasn't I informed?"

"It happened the night of Larson's psychotic break," Wright said. "Since then—"

"Yes, yes, never mind," Carol snapped. "So now we have *three* ghosts plaguing the ship. Dammit. Can Orr tell us anything?"

"I don't think so," said Wright. "I talked to her briefly after her suicide attempt. She seemed as ignorant as the rest of us. She might be able to help us more if she's allowed some human contact. She's in a bad way."

"My heart bleeds," Carol commented.

"The major has a point," said Kim. "From what I understand, Kala Orr was close to the alien, Morgan. If she were in a better psychological state she might remember something important, or if she's withholding information she might feel more inclined to help us."

"She nearly sabotaged the FTL drive!" exclaimed Carol. "I don't know how, but she managed to persuade two highly intelligent engineers to allow her into the operations room. If we let her loose again, who knows what she'll do?"

"I wasn't suggesting we give her complete freedom of movement," Kim replied, "but some time spent with other people wouldn't hurt. Orr's background is disturbing and complex. It isn't fair to hold her entirely accountable for her actions."

Wright was beginning to regret his suggestion. He had a horrible feeling about who would be keeping Orr company. Colbourn was looking at him.

"I think Orr needs professional help," he said, "from a professional." He turned his attention to Dr Kim.

"I am willing to visit Kala Orr," said Arthur. "We have both been tormented by the specters."

"She's terrified of you," Wright objected, though excluding Arthur meant the duty was more likely to fall to himself. "She thinks you're the only person who can kill her, and she might think you *want* to kill her."

"Then I can reassure her I don't."

"I'm not sure that'll help."

"I still say we've gotta turn back!" Grady argued. "I don't give a shit about the ex-Dwyr, and I don't give a shit about visiting a goddamned exoplanet. This trip is far too dangerous. I wasn't warned about ghosts or demented air force officers. If I'd known what might happen I never would have signed up. If we don't turn back right now, I'll sue the Alliance for every penny it has!"

Carol and Colbourn shared a smile.

"Mr Grady," Carol said condescendingly, "as I've explained, your opinion is irrelevant. If you wish to consult legal counsel upon our return, you are free to do so. But let me repeat, we are continuing with this mission. I have apprised the Prime Minister, Sea Lord, and Chief of Defence of everything that's happened, and my orders are to proceed as planned. London has spoken on the matter, and therefore all discussion on the subject is closed. I hope I make myself clear."

33

———

Wright set a mug of coffee in front of Iolani and sat down.

"Thanks."

"How are you doing?" asked Abacha.

They were in the mess between mealtimes, several days after the incident with Larson. Iolani didn't want to return to the briefing room, understandably.

"Okay," she replied, in a tone that implied she wasn't. She sipped her coffee before adding, "You know, I miss greenery... plants, trees. The Alliance should have included a biome on this ship. It might have helped to keep people sane."

"Something to put in your report when we get back," said Wright.

"*If* we get back," said Iolani.

"You seriously think we won't?" Abacha asked. "You guys have to tell me what's going on. Us lowly corporals don't hear anything. What happened at the meeting about the shooting?"

"Ugh," she said. "The usual. Carol throwing his weight around."

"Sounds familiar."

"He *is* in charge of the mission," said Wright gently. "If anyone should throw his weight around, it's him."

"The short version is," said Iolani, "we're continuing as normal, despite everything that's happened and might happen. I'm only hanging around with you guys from now on. You two don't seem as crazy as everyone else."

"Thanks for the compliment," Abacha said. "I'm not, but I can't speak for the major here."

"I'm definitely not less crazy than the average Royal Marine," said Wright. He was only partly joking. Ever since seeing the vision of his father, he'd been wondering about the state of his mind. Yet Arthur had seen the vision too.

"So have you been sentenced to spending time with Kala Orr?" Iolani asked him. "I saw Colbourn looking at you."

"You did? I got the impression she had me in her sights too, but, no, thank the stars, I've been spared that. Kim is giving her counseling sessions. I don't think it'll help, to be honest. She's too far gone. The poor woman's round the bend. But maybe she'll feel less alone."

"The poor woman?" Abacha echoed. "Are you feeling a smidgen of sympathy for her?"

Wright shrugged. "She must miss her son." He went to take a drink, but an alarm blared out.

"Shit," Abacha shouted over the noise. "What is it this time?"

"Maybe Kala Orr escaped," yelled Iolani.

They both looked to Wright for an explanation, but no orders or information had arrived via his implant.

"The door's locked," someone called out.

The speaker was standing at a closed door, dragging on the surface with his hands.

"So's this one!" exclaimed someone else.

Wright comm'd Colbourn.

"Stand by, Major," was all she said.

A cook wandered out from the kitchen and surveyed the mess, hands on hips. Someone approached her and Wright read her lips. She seemed to say, *Everything's dead.* He went over to her.

"What's wrong?" he asked.

"Nothing's working. Printers, ovens, dispensers, all kaput."

"You've lost power?"

"No, the power's there, lights are on, but nothing's working. I can't get into the fridges either. They better fix things quick or there'll be a mutiny. Nothing angrier than a hungry Marine."

The alarm blasted out three more times then fell silent.

Still, Colbourn told him nothing.

Quiet fell now the alarm had stopped. The people continued to try to open the doors, though their efforts were pointless. When a door on a starship was sealed, the only way through it was via molecular scalpel unless the seal deactivated.

Minutes crawled by, and no word from outside the mess arrived. Wright tried to exercise patience, putting off comming Colbourn again. She was probably dealing with a crisis and would contact him when she was ready. Tension tightened as the people grew concerned about being trapped.

"Hell, at least we have food and restrooms," someone quipped. "It could be worse."

No one laughed.

Finally, fifteen or so minutes later, the two mess doors opened.

"Major," said Colbourn. "Come to the bridge. I'll explain while you're on your way."

He said goodbye to Iolani and Abacha. As he jogged along the passageway, Colbourn said, "Something infiltrated the ship's systems. It was a massive breach. Swept right through everything, and there was nothing we could do to stop it."

"Everything?"

"Everything. Databases, weapons systems, cloaking device, EV control... The lot. We're completely vulnerable to attack. The Lieutenant-General is gathering all senior officers on the bridge to formulate a defense."

"A defense to what exactly?"

"Good question."

FOR THE FIRST TIME EVER, Wright saw concern in Lieutenant-General Carol's features. The man's ability to remain calm and optimistic was legendary. If *he* was worried, there was definitely something to be worried about.

He'd registered Wright when he arrived but immediately returned his focus to the comm console. The comms officer also watched the screen expectantly while also listening on his headset.

Colbourn approached.

"What's happening?" Wright asked her.

"We're waiting to hear from London."

"Carol asked for advice before taking evasive action?" he asked incredulously.

"What kind of evasive action would you suggest, Major? There's nothing out there. Scan data indicate the same vast vacuum speckled with tiny particles they always have. There's literally nothing to evade."

"Except this thing that ran through the ship like a dose of salts. *Something's* there. We just can't detect it."

"Yes, you're right. There has to be. The Lieutenant-General has asked permission to turn back."

"Ah, I see. Josh Grady will be pleased."

"He'll be pleased if we receive it. I've a funny feeling—"

"Sir," said the comms officer to Carol, "London wants to speak to you directly." He handed over his headset.

Carol frowned as he listened. He nodded once, then twice, then his shoulders sagged. "Yes, sir. I understand. I'll keep you up to date with any further developments." He listened again. "Thank you." He took off the headset and returned it.

Addressing the bridge, he said, "There is to be no deviation to our route. We are to proceed as planned. London is sending new code to update our system security."

A ripple of dismay passed through the room.

What good would new security code do when their attacker had swept through the old stuff like a scythe through grass?

"It's like going into battle unarmed with your pants around your ankles," someone remarked softly.

"Now then," said Carol. "I won't hear any grumbles. We have our orders and we will follow them. That's it. Back to your duties, everyone. Captain, put the crew on amber alert and tell the passengers to return to their cabins and remain there until further notice."

The captain, Throndsen, opened the shipwide comm and began to make the announcement.

34

A little over an hour later, when Wright had dared to hope the *Dauntless* wasn't about to come under attack, he noticed a smudge in the air. He was on the bridge, and the smudge seemed to be suspended midway between him and Carol.

At first, he thought he must have something in his eyes. He rubbed them and blinked, but the smudge remained.

It was getting brighter.

"Lieutenant-General," he said.

"Yes, Major?"

He pointed.

The spot had increased in luminosity even as he spoke. Carol didn't need any further prompting to see it.

"Good lord," he muttered.

Soon, everyone on the bridge was staring at the brightening, slim oval of light.

Wright's hand went to his beamer, but what was the point? How would a pulse round affect something made of energy?

"Whoa!" He took a step backward. The thing had suddenly

shifted shape into a humanoid form—a figure resembling his father.

"I've never seen one in the flesh, so to speak," said Carol. "Only recordings. This should be interesting."

It spoke, and this time the words could be heard, though it didn't sound anything like Wright's father. The voice seemed to come from far away, as if spoken from the end of a long passageway.

"TJ Wright, is this form pleasing to you?"

"*What*?"

A pause, and the thing slowly flickered like sunlight through leaves. "Does this appearance cause you distress?"

All gazes turned on him.

"Yes, actually, it does."

Instantly the light flattened to resume its oval shape, edges indistinct. "We can only use images known to you. Your senses do not perceive us. We apologize for disturbing you. Your minds are difficult for us to comprehend."

"I am Lieutenant-General Carol, and *I* am the one in charge here. Who are you? I demand on behalf of the Britannic Alliance that you reveal your identity."

The thing didn't move in response to Carol's statement. It could probably see or perceive everything around it.

"There is no word in any of your languages for what we are. Perhaps you would call us aliens, but that would not be correct."

"Why not?" asked Colbourn. "You're clearly an alien life form of some kind."

"Alien means not of your home planet."

"Then you're from Earth?" Colbourn asked.

"We are not from anywhere. We're from everywhere."

Carol stepped closer to the light and said, "Was it you who went through our ship's systems?"

"We needed a better understanding of your species and

methods of communication. Our previous attempts to communicate with you were unsuccessful. Now we have established contact, we will impart important information soon. We will return."

The light was gone.

"*Fuck*," someone breathed.

Wright could have said the same himself.

"Language, Marine," snapped Carol. He turned to Wright. "If it knows everything about us and the ship, it knows I'm the highest-ranking officer aboard and in charge of the mission. Why do you think it addressed *you* first?"

"Not a clue, sir."

"Hmm." Carol drummed his fingers on a console. "And before you it appeared to Arthur and Orr. Odd. The person it briefly resembled, that was your father?"

"Yes."

"Any idea why it picked him?"

"Absolutely none."

He turned to the captain. "The ship will remain on amber alert."

~

THE THING DIDN'T COME BACK.

Carol ordered that all the data from the moment of its appearance until it left was assessed, but all that could be found was the usual slightly higher electrical charge. The Lieutenant-General sent all the details to London, and the command to continue the mission returned. After twelve hours at amber alert, Carol downgraded the status to yellow, the passengers were allowed out of their cabins, and some semblance of normality returned.

Wright's duty hours were over. He returned to Arthur's cabin, exhausted by the events of the day. Though he hadn't done much, the reappearance of his 'father' and all the associated memories evoked had wrung his nerves. Then there was also the steady threat of attack from something they couldn't perceive that had infiltrated their systems like water soaking into a sponge.

The cabin was empty. Arthur was probably eating dinner with Iolani and Abacha.

He stripped off and stepped into the shower. Two minutes of hot water was all that was allowed for showers, so he made use of it, quickly lathering up. He was in the middle of shampooing his hair, his eyes closed, when a voice said, "Major Wright."

"*Shit!*"

It was the voice of the thing from the bridge.

His eyes opened reflexively and were instantly filled with soap.

"Arghh. What?!" he demanded. "What do you want?"

What was it about showers that attracted the thing's attention?

Rinsing his eyes with water, he blinked and squinted. The light hovered outside the stall.

Thanking the stars it didn't look like his dad, he repeated, "What do you want? You need to speak to Lieutenant-General Carol, not me. I'm not the one running the show around here."

"That person isn't important. The connections outside your star system run mainly to you and the two other humans we tried to contact."

"Connections? What connections?"

The hot water cut off. Half of his hair was full of shampoo.

"Look, can you wait until I get out of here?"

The light didn't answer.

He grabbed a towel and dried himself, rubbing his hair with distaste. He wrapped the towel around his waist and stepped out. The light was closer than he'd thought and he accidentally brushed against it. His skin tingled.

He edged around the glow and backed up to the washbasin.

"Can you listen now?" the light asked.

"I'm listening, but... Hold on a sec."

Feeling like he was in a vid drama written by someone on hallucinogens, he opened the door to the cabin, reached out to the nightstand and grabbed an interface. He turned on the recorder. "Go ahead."

"Your language is very limited, but we will try to explain. Your species doesn't seem to see the connections. Your transportation isn't following the paths. It is severing and damaging the lines."

"Uhh, you're right. I have no idea what you're talking about and I'm not sure even our physicists would either. But we have some aboard. You should talk to them. Maybe they'll understand what you mean better than me."

"We are preparing a detailed explanation and will insert it into your database. We will try to communicate to you more simply."

"Thanks, but I'm just a Marine. I'm not important. I don't need to know this stuff." He wanted the thing to go away. Aside from the possibility of it turning into one of his parents, he didn't want to put Carol's nose out of joint by being the object of the newcomer's attention.

"You are important," said the light. "You need to understand. Listen. All things in the universe are connected. Every atom, molecule, compound, and substance is connected by pathways your species does not perceive yet. You are at an early stage of evolution. Most paths form naturally, others are forged by actions. There are paths leading to and from your star system that were forged by actions, even though you are the first humans to leave it. Another species has visited your system, has it not?"

"Yes, it has," Wright replied, guessing Merlin and Morgan were the 'other species'. "At least, that's what we think happened."

"The connections from outside the system run strongly to you personally, and more so to the humans called Arthur and Kala Orr."

"I think I'm beginning to understand. So you can see these connections outside our ship?"

"'See' is not the correct word, but, yes, we can 'see' them everywhere."

"And you've been trying to tell us to stop our ship from breaking them?"

"No. We would prefer you did not break them but they will naturally repair. Though you should know you are expending excessive amounts of energy unnecessarily."

"Then why do you want to talk to me in particular?"

"We want to warn you. The other species who invaded your system is far in advance of yours. It possesses knowledge you do not. It is playing along the lines while yours is blundering about like a...a toddler. Does that make sense to you?"

"Kind of. You wanted to talk to me or Arthur or Kala because you see lots of these action-based lines leading to us? We've only just become aware of what the aliens were doing. That's one reason we decided to leave our system and explore outside."

"You are taking the first step of a long journey. We wish you luck."

The light seemed about to depart.

"Wait," said Wright, "this other species that's playing with us, what can you tell me about them? How can we stop their interference? Are they breaking galactic laws?"

"There are no galactic laws. We only saw a new, young life form and felt inclined to help it. Some of us believe we were once like you, a very long time ago."

"Can you tell me more about your kind? How come our scanners don't pick you up? Do you travel in starships?"

"So curious. So much to learn. It is refreshing to discover what is in your mind. But we cannot answer your questions in terms you would understand. We have fulfilled our desire to warn you and adjust the balance a little in your favor. We will input an information packet into your—"

"There has to be something you can tell me to help us fight the aliens threatening us."

"We suggest you don't fight them. They are far more powerful than you."

"But—"

The light went out.

35

———

"**I** only want the ability to move freely around the ship," Kala said. "I don't think that's too much to ask. I've been locked in this horrible cell for months."

She bit her lip. Was she pushing too hard? The psychiatrist's reactions were difficult to read.

Dr Kim replied smoothly, "You know the reason for your incarceration. What you did posed a danger to the safety of everyone aboard."

"But I didn't do anything! I only wanted to understand how the FTL drive works. Who better to explain it to me than the people who operate it? Is it my fault they invited me into the control room? I didn't touch a thing, and suddenly I found myself being hauled out of there like a common criminal."

Kim gave her a knowing look.

"I didn't *do* anything," Kala reiterated sullenly. "Since when has it been legal to lock someone up for months for simply being where they weren't supposed to be?"

"We're aboard a military ship operating under military regulations. I'm not sure what rules you set in place for the

EAC, but in the Alliance the military aren't governed by the same laws as the general populace. If you wish to make a complaint to the authorities on our return—"

"*If* we ever return from this godforsaken trip." She took a breath and let it out evenly. Staying calm was difficult. She hadn't wanted to come on this mission in the first place. She hadn't wanted to leave Perran alone. Not only did she miss him badly, he was too young and easy to manipulate. Naturally, that was the whole point. While she was gone, the Alliance would be rolling back everything she'd done in her days in power, undoing all her good work, returning civilization to its reliance on technology and orthodox physics.

"The worst thing about being here is not knowing what's happening," she said. "No one tells me anything."

"What would you like to know?"

"John hasn't been back for weeks. Has something changed?"

"John?"

"The apparition that appeared to me took the form of an old friend."

"Ah, yes. The visits prompted your suicide attempt. They must have been very disturbing for you. Would you like to tell me more about that?"

"No! I..." Kala seethed. She imagined strangling the doctor, seeing the veins swell in her neck, her eyes pop from her skull. "I don't have anything to say. It was hard for me, mostly because I'm locked in here day and night. If I could just be allowed out for a short time, an hour or two. If I stayed under armed guard, I couldn't hurt anyone, could I? What could I possibly do? And it would make me feel so much better."

"Well," said Kim, looking down at her interface, "I suppose it wouldn't hurt to request a short period of freedom for mental health reasons. Being deprived of human contact *is* psychologically damaging."

"Thank you," said Kala, trying to sound grateful though the words scoured her throat. "If you could request it for me, I would appreciate it so much."

Kim looked up and smiled. "Certainly."

36

The astrophysicists were deeply excited by the information and formulae files that had appeared in the *Dauntless*'s database. That was what Wright heard secondhand, anyhow, through Colbourn. The scientists relayed the information to their colleagues on Earth and consulted with them for long hours about what it all meant. Colbourn said they estimated human understanding of universal laws had leapt a thousand years ahead.

He'd sent the recording of his conversation with the light to Carol and, after debriefing, he lay low, avoiding the Lieutenant-General's wounded ego. The fact that the aliens had elected to reveal the secrets of the universe to an officer several ranks below him had to hurt, especially for someone who had as high an opinion of himself as Carol did.

Wright often thought over what the light had told him but he couldn't make much of it except that it chimed in somewhat with things Arthur had said.

His father didn't put in any more appearances, and Guinevere seemed to have given up on haunting Arthur, so he returned to his old cabin.

Life went on.

The *Dauntless* had covered four-fifths of the distance to her destination. When the mood took him, Wright would check what was happening on Earth, especially in the BI. Generally, it was good news. The damage Orr had done was being fixed. Roads were rebuilt, public facilities re-opened, the economy re-ignited. His homeland didn't seem to be suffering for the lack of an on-site monarch. Perran Orr was rarely in the news, though he remained a figurehead for the die-hard Crusaders.

War crimes trials had taken place. Kala Orr was lucky in that respect. For now, she'd escaped legal retribution for all the terrible things she'd done, all the abuses of human rights and conventions governing military conflict. Her name was often mentioned in the trials as part of the accused's defense of 'only following orders', but the courts couldn't try her personally in her absence. BI law didn't allow it. Parliament could have amended the statute but it didn't, perhaps unwilling to risk inflaming Crusaders' anger and jeopardizing the fragile harmony of the multicultural society.

So Orr was safe for the moment. What might happen upon the *Dauntless*'s return was another matter.

To pass the time, Wright had asked Arthur to teach him how to fight with staves.

The ease with which the king beat him again and again was somewhat demoralizing, but he persevered. It was better to lose to Arthur at fighting than Abacha at xiangqi. Arthur didn't gloat.

"Do you believe Merlin now?" the king asked one day as they were in the middle of a practice session.

He drove his staff at Wright's midriff. Wright twisted to one side just in time and the weapon pistoned in and out of empty space.

Arthur wanted to talk *and* spar? He must be finding it boring. They'd been going at it for fifteen minutes, the longest match they'd ever had. Wright had thought he'd been making headway, but maybe not.

"About what?" he asked, bringing his staff in an arcing sweep aimed below the king's left ear.

"His patterns," Arthur replied, ducking and leaping back. "You were skeptical, and Taylan didn't believe me either." He swiped at Wright's calves.

Wright jumped. As he landed, he leaned in and jerked his staff upward toward Arthur's chin, but the king smoothly turned his head to the side and drove a shoulder into Wright's chest, unbalancing him.

Wright stumbled backward and landed on his back. The king brought his staff down like an ax, as if to chop into Wright's skull, but at the last minute he slowed it almost to a stop and gently tapped Wright's sparring helmet. He held out a hand to help him up.

"You over-committed," he said. "Sometimes you have to jump, but you should never lose a firm setting on two feet if you can help it. Not unless you're confident you're landing a match-ending blow."

"I was *pretty* confident," Wright replied, panting. Arthur was correct, but he wasn't taking into account Wright's many hours of hand-to-hand combat training. He knew about over-committing. Putting the knowledge into practice when working with a new weapon was another thing entirely.

Arthur smiled and clapped him on the shoulder.

As they walked to the equipment storage room, Wright said, "I couldn't trust anything Merlin said. Why would I? He was as slippery as an eel."

"Now *that's* a comparison I can understand. He was indeed a slippery character, and still is, no doubt."

"But since the light told me about the lines and how they run to you, me, and Orr, I can see now he wasn't lying. Or at least he was partly telling the truth. His species must be able to perceive the connections. Taylan knows about them too?" Wright took off his helmet and stowed it along with his staff on the shelves.

Arthur did the same. "I tried to convince her that Merlin was right about patterns governing people and events, and that if we paid attention to them we might find her children. She didn't believe me at first, but I think she may now."

"She did find her kids in the end with your help."

Arthur sighed. "I'm sure she's significant. That was why I wanted her to come along on the mission."

"Significant how?"

"The lines that link to us must also link to Taylan."

"I suppose so."

"TJ, Merlin and Morgan's game isn't over. It continues. We know this because Merlin said he would be back. If all things are connected as the specter said, we're still part of their game. Only now, by coming out here, we aren't passive anymore. We aren't pawns, we're players. Taylan has been a part of everything since the beginning. I believe she's a player too. But she's months away. What if something happens and she isn't here? We'll be at a disadvantage."

"She's more than months away," Wright replied. Arthur *really* didn't understand about FTL travel. "Maybe you're right, but it can't be helped. She isn't here and there's nothing we can do about it."

They went into the showers.

37

For the first time in the *Dauntless*'s long, long journey, the scanners had picked up something that wasn't space dust, a rogue planet, or a comet on an eons-long voyage from a distant sun.

It was another ship.

Data was still arriving when Wright stepped onto the bridge.

"She's heading straight for us," said an officer, Blake, before also stating the vessel's speed.

"That matches ours," Carol commented. "Stands to reason the ship has an FTL drive, out here in the middle of nowhere. Can you extrapolate back from her trajectory?" he asked. "Do we know where she's from?"

Wright had had the same thought. Was the starship from the system they were heading toward? Had the *Dauntless* been spotted and were beings from the exoplanet traveling out to meet the new arrival halfway? Had they decided the best form of defense was to attack?

"Working on it, sir," Blake replied.

The delay meant the new ship couldn't be from their destination. They were so close now, the computer would generate the information in microseconds. So if no carbon-dioxide-breathing aliens were approaching to greet/annihilate them, who could it be?

"Well?" Carol demanded.

"Sorry, sir. Still working on it."

"Should I try to hail them?" the comms officer asked.

Carol frowned. "I suppose it's worth a try. Give only our ship's name, however. Nothing more."

The comms officer complied. "This is the HMSS *Dauntless* hailing the approaching vessel. Please state your designation and purpose." When no reply came, Carol told her to continue to broadcast the message across all frequencies.

There was only silence from the other ship.

"Maybe we should try the new instant comm," Wright suggested.

Carol nodded. "Go ahead," he added to comms.

But if the approaching ship had entangled comm receivers, her occupants either didn't understand the message or didn't want to answer it.

"The chances their technology is similar to ours is remote," said Carol. "Trying to speak to them is a waste of breath. We can only see what they do when they get here. Do we have any idea where they're from yet?"

Blake replied, "They must have taken an indirect route from their home system, sir. The computer's showing nothing on their trail for thousands of light years."

"Okay, it doesn't make a difference, I suppose, though it would be nice to know where the buggers are from."

"Sir..." said Blake hesitantly, looking up with concern from his screen.

"Spit it out, man," Carol urged.

"Their ship's specs... They're remarkably similar to ours."

"They're...?"

"Dimensions and mass, she even *looks* like the *Dauntless*, sir. I can show you."

Blake activated the holo display, lighting up the center of the bridge.

"That's *her*?" asked Carol.

All attention was on the image of the vessel that hung in midair. If anyone had asked Wright to put a name to the ship, he would have said it was the *Dauntless*.

"You're sure that isn't a mistake?" Carol asked.

Blake replied, "Absolutely not. That's the vessel approaching us."

"But that isn't possible," said the comms officer, speaking for everyone.

Seconds ticked past as shock permeated the room.

Blake asked, "Could it be *us*, heading back?"

"No, that's ridiculous," said Carol.

Wright wasn't so sure. The information the astrophysicists had received had blown apart their understanding of the universe. Perhaps it was possible that time didn't work as it was generally accepted to work. The *Dauntless* approaching from another time seemed as plausible an explanation for what was happening as any other. If it wasn't the *Dauntless*, how could another life form have built a mirror image? *Why* would aliens build an exact copy of a strange ship?

"Whatever she is," said Carol, "we must be prepared for every eventuality, including an attack. If she *is* an identical copy of the *Dauntless*, at least we know exactly what she's capable of. Throndsen, turn off the FTL drive and activate our cloaking device. Let's see what our anonymous visitor does. Comms, sound battle stations."

"Aye aye, sir."

Carol told the captain to prepare for battle. "You know the score," he added. "I'll leave the details to you."

The captain nodded. They were in capable hands, the best

in the space fleet as far as Wright knew. He was glad Carol hadn't allowed his ego to get in the way of allowing Throndsen free rein.

Wright fastened his safety harness.

The pilot reported the ship had dropped out of light speed.

"They've done the same!" Blake blurted. "The other ship's now traveling the same speed as us."

Wright hadn't felt a thing. The thrusters had maintained the same speed, only now the *Dauntless* wasn't contained within a skin of warped space.

"Same trajectory?" Carol asked Blake.

"Yes, sir. Still coming straight at us."

"Activating cloak," said the pilot.

"Alter course," said Throndsen, giving a new heading.

An odd hush settled over the bridge. Though, again, there were no tangible effects on the ship's interior now she was cloaked, the people aboard got the sense they were hiding and should be quiet.

Wright was reminded of the attack of the *Gallant* on Kala Orr's flagship and waiting with Taylan, Arthur, and Merlin while Marines died in the fight to board her.

"Any updates, Blake?" Carol asked tersely.

Staring at his screen, he answered, "No, s—" He gasped. "We've lost them. No readings at all."

"They've cloaked too," said Carol. "I suppose we could have predicted it. Now it's the blind chasing the invisible."

"Yes," Throndsen agreed. "We can't see them, but they can't see us either. We should be able to avoid an engagement. With millions of square kilometers of space to search, they'll never find us."

"Sir," said Wright.

"Yes, Major?"

"Can I suggest we prepare for boarding?"

"Why? Throndsen is entirely correct. It would be impossible to locate us now."

"I can't explain why, sir," said Wright, "or not quickly anyway. I have a feeling it would be wise to be ready, just in case."

"Major, if they can find us to board us, they can also fire on us."

"Yes, sir. But there isn't a lot I can do about that."

Also, it isn't their style. If it is who I think it is, they'll want to play with us first.

"Well, it won't hurt. The crew are due a practice drill. Go ahead."

He unfastened his harness and began issuing commands as he ran from the bridge. Then he comm'd Arthur and told him to meet him at the aft airlock.

A thousand alarm bells were going off in his head. The situation was peculiar. A ship that was an exact copy of the *Dauntless*? And clearly stalking them, copying their every move? It was like the time after Kala Orr's failed victory parade, when, by some fluke, Merlin, Morgan, Orr, Arthur, Taylan, and he had all ended up in the same room together. Colbourn had been there too, and Hans Jonte, though he wasn't sure if they mattered.

The 'game' the aliens had been playing with human lives had reached some kind of denouement then, according to Merlin.

Was this the next stage?

He raced to the nearest armory.

38

———

"**I** think you're right, TJ," said Arthur as they waited at the aft hatch. He wasn't in armor and he was carrying his sword, not a pulse rifle.

Wright felt uneasy about the king's lack of protection, but he'd insisted that was how he wanted to fight, if it came to a fight. Maybe whatever Merlin had done to make him impervious to pulse rounds still applied, but what would the king do if the ship depressurized?

"Right about thinking we'll be boarded?"

"Yes."

Wright didn't answer. He hoped he was wrong. Having Arthur's agreement only made him more worried he wasn't.

The Marines were in place. All the *Dauntless*'s airlocks were covered. Carol had ordered the passengers to return to their cabins and lock themselves in. Whatever happened, they'd done their best to prepare.

He had Abacha with him. The man's presence on the ship was a double-edged sword. He was an excellent Marine, but Wright always dreaded the prospect of having to explain to

Taylan that her best friend had fallen in combat under his command. He wanted to keep him by his side.

They waited, lined up each side of the hatch and, farther back, across the passageway.

Wright stared at the closed lock door. If, as he suspected, the aliens who had been on Earth in the forms of Merlin and Morgan were about to attack, would they appear in human form or in their natural bodies? What did they look like? What weapons would they be carrying?

Booted feet came running up behind him.

He swiveled his head.

"Reporting for duty, Major."

He scanned his HUD. It was Commander Ryan Fletcher of the Navy, armored up.

It was a noble gesture but the man had never trained with the Royal Marines. "Thanks, Fletcher, but—."

"I'm not sitting in my cabin twiddling my thumbs while others fight to defend me."

Wright nodded. He got it. "Get to the back and try not to trip anyone up."

"Yes, sir."

"Major Wright," came one-to-one comm.

It was Major-General Bobbin. "Yes, ma'am?"

"Just to let you know I'm at the starboard airlock."

Another hero. Though she was Army she exceeded him in rank and wasn't about to show him the deference Fletcher had.

"Copy." He cut the comm. If non-Marine military wanted to help repel boarders it was up to them. He wasn't going to argue about it. They might need everyone they had.

Arthur scanned the overhead and up and down the passageway. "How will we know when they're coming?"

"Could be a few things," Wright replied, "but, don't worry, we'll know."

The words were barely out of his mouth when the *Dauntless* shuddered.

"Something like *that*," he added before switching to a general comm to his Marines. "Weapons at the ready."

Every rifle lifted.

Carol comm'd him. "Unfortunately, you were correct, Major. Something has fastened onto us. Whatever it is, it's cloaked. We can't get any data except hull readings. I'm loath to pull away without knowing for sure we won't rip off our hull in the process. For the moment, it's down to you."

"Yes, sir."

When Merlin had arrived at the *Valiant* in his black cloud, he hadn't come aboard until they opened an airlock. Wright hoped that was because he couldn't, not because he was being polite. If the aliens toying with them could enter through garbage chutes and every other sealed gap in the hull, they were truly screwed.

A faint, metallic wrenching reached his ears. He turned up his helmet's audio. The sound was unmistakable. The aliens were forcing the airlock.

An alarm blasted out and echoed down the passageway.

Tension passed along the waiting lines of Marines. Wright peeked through the hatch window. There was no corresponding window on the outer hatch. He could only watch until...

The outer hatch split from its surround, moved inward and then to one side. For a brief moment, stars shone through the breach, then they were darkened. A black cloud oozed in, filling the empty space. The cloud grew even darker, coalesced, and turned into a human form.

Wright swallowed. "It's Merlin," he told Arthur.

He stepped back from the window, adding, "He doesn't seem to be armed."

"Maybe he only wishes to speak to us."

"I doubt it."

Arthur ran his gaze down his sword's edge. "I enjoyed cutting off his head. I would enjoy doing it again."

"Arthur, he's going to break through the inner hatch, and then this passageway will lose air and anyone not magnetized to the deck will be sucked out into space. You need to leave, now."

"Merlin won't allow that to happen. Not at first anyway. I think he sees me as his favorite hound."

Wright wished he had Arthur's confidence. On the other hand, Arthur *had* known Merlin a long time.

The inner hatch began to move, sinking into the bulkhead as Merlin drew it into the airlock. Depressurization alarms resounded, louder than the hull breach ones. Figures on Wright's HUD dropped into the red zone. All around, the exits from the passageway would be sealing.

He glanced at Arthur. His hair had been whipped forward and covered his face, but, miraculously, the man was standing his ground against the departing rush of air.

Merlin stepped into view.

He was wearing the same long gown and tight-fitting cap he'd worn when Wright had first seen him. And the same supercilious smile.

"Arthur." He nodded. "Major Wright, it's a pleasure to see you again."

How could he see his face behind his darkened visor?

How could his voice pass through the vacuum?

"I can't say the same," Wright replied. "Leave this ship, or prepare to be ejected."

Merlin's smile grew wider.

He had just broken into the ship as easily as a kid opening a Christmas present. If he wanted to kill everyone aboard, he didn't need to go to this trouble. He was toying with them.

He moved to one side.

A second Merlin walked in from the airlock, identical in every way to the first.

Wright took another step back.

Up and down the passageway, Marines sent their comrades glances as if checking they were all seeing the same thing.

The two Merlins stepped apart. A third figure appeared from the airlock: Morgan. Her twin joined her.

"Yeah, nice magic trick," Wright growled. "Now get out."

But the first Merlin moved closer to him. "I admire your weapon, Major. Is that what you call a pulse rifle? I wouldn't mind having one of my own."

He reached behind his back and pulled a rifle from nowhere.

Laughing maniacally, he aimed the muzzle directly at Wright's visor.

Wright fired.

The round hit Merlin square in the stomach, opening it like a ripe peach. But, unlike when Arthur had decapitated him, no blood came out. He bent his head toward the gaping hole, through which his copy was visible behind him.

Then he evaporated into smoke, instantly whipped away by the vacuum.

Wright backed up some more.

Another Merlin appeared from the airlock, already armed.

Suddenly, they were all carrying rifles.

They started firing.

Arthur ran forward. He sliced through a Morgan's neck, but his sword had no effect. The cut closed as if it had never existed. He swung the blade through a Merlin, chopping from his shoulder down to his navel, but the creature didn't react and the wound sealed instantly.

The aliens were not firing at Arthur. Wright guessed they knew their pulse rounds wouldn't affect him. It was one of the rules of their bizarre game.

"Fire!" he ordered. "Weapons free."

The rounds destroyed every Merlin or Morgan they hit, but each was quickly replaced. His Marines didn't have the same protection as Arthur. The pulses fired by the invaders began to have a devastating effect. His men and women were suffering under the barrage from ever-increasing aliens.

And there was nowhere to fall back to. They couldn't leave the passageway while it was open to space without further depressurization.

It was win here or die trying.

39

Kala Orr giggled. It had been so easy. The stupid psychiatrist had been as easy to manipulate as the FTL operators. Morgan had told her once it was people with flexible thinking who were the most malleable, and it was true. Dr Kim was willing to entertain too many possibilities. Her sense of morality was complex. The question of allowing a little freedom to someone who had threatened the safety of the ship was not black and white to her.

Kala leaned out from her hiding place, breathless after her run. She'd taken off in the opposite direction the moment the doctor's back was turned. She giggled again at the memory.

She was free!

Of course, the ship being under attack helped. Everyone would have better things to do than find her. The military men and women were focused on defense and the passengers had retreated to their cabins.

She had the run of the ship.

What should she do? Where should she go?

The FTL operators were unlikely to allow her into the control room again. Even *they* could not be quite so dumb. It would be delightful to go to the bridge and shoot down Carol, Colbourn, and every officer there, but she had no weapon and the armories would be busy with people. Maybe she should murder a few passengers. Ha! That would be fun to do while everyone's back was turned. Even if the Alliance won the battle, they would have some sad discoveries to ruin their victory celebrations.

But, realistically, who would allow her into their cabin? And as soon as she was seen, she would give away her location. She had to stay hidden as long as possible.

The mess? She could contaminate the food with something poisonous.

That was no good. She wanted immediate gratification, not to sit in her cell and hope no one noticed what she'd done. She wanted to witness her revenge. She wanted to see and feel the blood of her victim.

Ah! I know just the place.

40

———

In the midst of the firefight, an expected comm arrived: "Starboard airlock breached, sir."

Wright told his lieutenant what to expect.

He didn't know what else to say to him. They were in a tight spot themselves. The Merlins and Morgans seemed endless. No matter how many they shot down, more appeared. He guessed the vapor they dissolved into when pulse rounds hit them recondensed elsewhere and reformed into a new attacker.

Meanwhile, his own Marines didn't have the same option. Several were down already, the dots representing them turning blue on his HUD. *They* would not be coming back.

Arthur was in the midst of the aliens, swinging his sword like a machete, hacking into them desperately. Sweat soaked the man's shirt and coated his face. He wouldn't give up, though his efforts were pointless.

"SITREP, Major." It was Carol.

"We're holding them off for now, sir. I don't know how much longer we'll last. They have infinite backup from the look of it."

"I see. The situation is the same at the starboard airlock."

"I know, sir. Any suggestions would be welcome."

"The physicists are working on it. They're studying your feed, trying to figure out a weakness in these aliens we can exploit. I'll let you know as soon as they have anything."

It was something. If anyone could understand a way to defeat the Merlins and Morgans, surely scientists could, especially now they were armed with new knowledge.

Agony stabbed his side.

He'd been hit.

The moment's inattention to deal with Carol's comm had been his undoing. The Morgan who had fired on him fell, her head destroyed. The black mist rose from her body and dissipated.

The passageway, scorched, scored, and smoking from pulse fire, wavered in his vision. He blinked and it swam back into focus. Pressure hypodermics in his armor pressed into his skin and the pain of his wound faded, though he could still smell his burned flesh.

The aliens occupied the central section of passageway—he estimated twenty to twenty-five of them. The churn of them falling, vaporizing, and reappearing was confusing. The Marines had been pushed backward into each end. The men and women in the rear were literally thrust against the sealed exits, unable to fire for fear of hitting their comrades.

If things continued as they were, the Merlins and Morgans would slowly but surely kill every last one of them.

"TJ!" Arthur roared, whirling his sword. "We must do something or your ship will be lost."

I know.

But what?

A Merlin ran out of the bunch, his face wild-eyed and wreathed in a cadaver-like grin. The tip of Arthur's sword sliced uselessly through his neck. Wright aimed, but before he fired the Merlin got his own shot out. A Marine at Wright's side took the hit on his visor. At the close range, the visor was destroyed.

"Get back!" Wright screamed. "To the rear, Marine!"

He fought the urge to vomit, the image of Patel's ruined face stark in his mind.

He fired.

The round ripped a hole in the Merlin's chest. The creature fell backward, already dissolving before it hit the deck. A Morgan was behind him. Wright stepped forward and fired again, blowing her head off.

"Advance!" he yelled. "Give them everything you've got!"

It was their only hope. They had to force every last one of the aliens off the ship. They had to kill them faster than they could regenerate. They had to seal the airlocks somehow, detach from the other ship, get away…

It was hopeless and he knew it. Better to go down fighting than to die from a shot in the back.

He fired again, and again, and again.

The Marines surged forward. The helmets of those at the other end of the passageway appeared through the Morgans and Merlins. They began to gain ground. A barrage of pulse fire flew from their rifles. At this rate, they would run out of energy soon, but what did it matter? What was the point of conserving it when they were fighting for their lives?

A haze began to build up as smoke from the burned bulkheads and evaporating aliens' bodies increased faster than the vapors disappeared into space.

A pulse exploded against him and once more agony flooded his body. He staggered. The shot had hit his left shoulder. He continued firing, cradling his rifle in his right arm. He would get a second dose of painkillers but that would be it. Painful seconds seemed to drag out until the drugs finally hit his bloodstream.

A Marine fell at his feet. He stepped over the prone figure.

How many Morgans and Merlins now? Ten? Fifteen?

A Morgan danced toward him mockingly. "Major Wright?

Where's my darling Kala Orr? She's aboard this ship, isn't she? I can feel her."

He shot her in the face.

He took a third hit.

His hip was on fire.

He fell to his knees.

"TJ?"

He couldn't answer.

"TJ?"

"Arthur, I can't..."

"It isn't Arthur, it's Iolani. I asked Lieutenant-General Carol to patch me through."

"Uhuh." His hip was a ball of pain. The analgesics didn't touch it.

"I had an idea."

A Merlin was bearing down on him. He weakly lifted his rifle.

The alien moved in and out of focus.

He fired.

The Merlin crumpled and fell, but Wright fell too. The deck rose up to meet his face.

"We're going to try foam."

Foam?

He waited for the kill shot. All that was needed was a single round, point blank range, to the back of his helmet.

But instead he heard a hiss from overhead.

Foam exploded on the deck next to his face. Pressure and the ship's a-grav was forcing it downward despite the pull of the vacuum.

We're going to try foam.

They'd activated the fire-extinguishing system for the passageway. Would it work?

Fighting the pain radiating through him, he turned and lifted his head. A Merlin was dissolving, but as it did so, foam sprayed through its cloud, destroying it. The black vapor didn't make it out the airlock. A faint, dark gray stain formed where the Merlin had been.

The other aliens saw what was happening and hesitated.

The Marines were hesitating too, confused by the sudden appearance of the foam.

"Fire on them," Wright commanded. "Fire on the fuckers."

It was the last thing he remembered.

 hand rested on his forehead.

He opened his eyes.

"Arthur?"

The hand moved away.

The king looked older than ever, and melancholy lay behind his eyes though he was smiling. "I'm glad you're finally awake."

The gentleness of his gesture, touching Wright's forehead, was typical of him. Somehow, the king managed to do things like that without seeming unmanly. It set him apart from this time.

Wright tried to move but found he couldn't. He looked down. Dressings swathed the part of his torso visible above the bed sheet. He turned his head. He was in sick bay. "We won?"

"The battle, not the war."

"Thank the stars." He closed his eyes. "I really thought we'd had it."

"It was close. If Iolani hadn't come up with her suggestion…"

"I was all out of ideas. How to defeat something that doesn't

—or can't—die? Fire-extinguishing foam. Who would have thought it could be something so simple?"

"I should have thought of it myself," said Arthur. "Rain washes dust from the air. Even I know that. All we needed was something to destroy the black clouds."

"You know plenty of things no one else can even guess at these days. Things we forgot long ago."

"Perhaps."

"What's happened to their ship?"

"Teams are working on it at the moment, figuring out if we can attach her to the *Dauntless* and take her home with us."

"*Huh*?"

"After the last Merlin and Morgan left, Lieutenant-General Carol took an educated guess at where the mirror ship sat and fired on her with the new weapon."

"The EMP emitter?"

"If that's what it's called."

"We knocked out their electronics? Fantastic."

"The cloak over their ship failed and we could board her."

"Let me guess. It was empty."

Arthur smiled. "You are correct. The Merlins and Morgans had deserted her. I'm not sure why."

"Maybe they were worried we'd be carrying super soakers."

"Super soakers? Is that a kind of gun? Anyway, I don't think so. It's probably something to do with their game." His smile grew wider. "I think we won this round."

"I think we did."

They laughed, but it made Wright's shoulder hurt so he quickly stopped.

"Was their ship the same as ours on the inside too?" he asked.

"I heard it *looked* the same. I expect others can answer you better than I."

Their conversation paused as Wright gathered courage. "Do you know how many we lost?"

Arthur looked down. "Nineteen altogether. Seventeen Marines, Commander Fletcher, and the passenger Josh Grady."

"Grady? How did he die? Did he get caught in crossfire? He should have stayed in his cabin."

"He was at the starboard airlock with Bobbin."

"He was fighting? Damn. She shouldn't have let him."

"Perhaps, but it's hard to deny a valorous request."

"Major." Colbourn's hard, clipped tones cut through the friendly atmosphere. She came up behind Arthur and when she reached him she silently gave him a hard stare.

"I'd better let you rest," said Arthur.

Even the King of the Britannic Isles quailed under the brigadier's negative attention.

"Major Wright," she said after Arthur left, her tone softened almost to kindness, "I'm glad you made it. How are you feeling? Not in too much pain I hope?"

"I'm okay, ma'am."

"Excellent. The doctor expects you'll be up and around in forty-eight hours. The healing gels are remarkable."

She sat down, and Wright's heart sank. She clearly planned on sticking around. Fatigue was catching up with him and he would rather have gone back to sleep.

"Major, your performance during this mission has been exemplary. You have demonstrated exceptional courage, initiative, and leadership. I am recommending you for promotion."

"Thank you, ma'am, but I was actually thinking of—"

She held up a hand to silence him. "Before you say anything, please listen. Physicists on Earth have been working on the information packet we sent them. As you know, considerably more time has passed there than we've experienced while traveling at light speed. Without any exaggeration, it seems the information has lifted humanity's understanding of the physical universe to an entirely new level. We know vastly more than we could have expected to discover for centuries."

Apparently in reaction to his underwhelmed expression, she continued in a heavier tone, "The Alliance has begun construction of a vessel containing a new drive that can exploit this new knowledge. The engineers refer to it as 'moving along the skeins', or some such phrase. It doesn't matter. The point is, after a reasonable period of recuperation, we would like you to—"

"Ma'am, I really feel I've done more than my duty in helping the Alliance's cause."

"You have," she answered gravely. "I'm not denying it. More than anyone could reasonably expect. However, it turns out what the light told you is true. You are already deeply involved in this conflict going on between us and the aliens who infiltrated our planet long ago. And so are many others. Taylan Ellis, for example."

"Arthur was right?"

"Arthur was entirely right."

"*Damn.*"

"This new knowledge we have doesn't take away our free will. You can always refuse, but, well, the understanding the implication of your refusal is unavoidable. I have thought it over myself and I feel I don't actually have much choice."

"You're involved too?"

She nodded and then stood up. "I'll leave you in peace. Think it over. You have plenty of time. We have a long return journey ahead of us."

"We aren't going to the planet anymore?"

"There's no longer any point. Not now we understand what's happening."

HE MUST HAVE DOZED OFF.

All he knew was he couldn't breathe. A hand was clamped over his mouth and nose.

Kala Orr was looking down at him, her eyes manic and inhuman, her mouth open and curved into a rictus.

He struggled, but she was up on his bed, her knee on his chest. He couldn't throw her off. He was too weak and in too much pain.

"Oh yes, Major Wright," she hissed. "Not so confident now, are we? Not so brave, manhandling a woman. How does it feel now the tables are turned? Now *I'm* the one in power over *you*."

Her mad grin deepened and her eyes flashed. "I might not rule my domain anymore. I might have been torn from my child. But I can still get my revenge. I can still see the blood of at least one of my enemies, and I will!"

She lifted a scalpel in her other hand. Its blade glinted. "Not very big, is it? I would prefer something longer and the time to slowly flay you alive. But it's long enough to reach the artery in your neck. Goodbye, Major Wright!"

A tall figure swooped in. Large hands grasped Orr's arms and lifted her bodily off the bed.

Wright gasped as he breathed again.

Arthur had her.

She fought him, kicking, biting, and scratching, but she was no match for the powerful man. He fastened her in a bear hug, her back against his chest and her feet off the floor, ignoring the blows from her heels.

"Dear wife," he said into her ear, "I thought you might try something like this. I would gladly slit your throat for trying to kill my friend, but sadly you're still important in this game we must play. Come with me."

He winked at Wright and carried her away.

42

A flower seller had set up a shop on the street, her wares stacked in bundles or crammed into buckets of water. Sweet fragrances filled the air. The seller sat on a low stool in the midst of the delicate petals and beautiful hues wearing clothes that mimicked their shades. Her garb reminded Wright of the outfit Taylan had worn when she'd masqueraded as a fortune teller, when the BI had been under Kala Orr's tyrannical rule and she'd spread her backwards misery over the land.

How desperate and sad Taylan had been, deep down, in those days. She'd covered it up with hostility and aloofness. As her commanding officer he should have seen it. He should have seen something was wrong.

"Flowers, sir?" the seller asked.

He realized he'd been standing looking at them for several minutes.

"Something for a loved one, or," she added, winking, "someone you *want* to love you?"

"I'll take those," he replied, pointing at a bunch of pink and yellow blooms.

The seller wrapped the flowers in a sheet of paper from the stack at her feet and handed them over. Wright looked for her credchip scanner.

"Cash only, sir."

He dug in his pocket. He'd been warned about this at the spaceport and had withdrawn a stash of paper notes from his account.

During his onward journey, he'd noticed the Isles had become a strange place in his absence. It hadn't entirely reverted to the BI he'd grown up in, a modern nation with modern systems and conveniences. It was an amalgam of the old and the new. The Crusaders had been allowed to retain their practices and beliefs with the exception that their children had to attend state schools and receive orthodox medical care. Though it was often subtle, the influence of the cultists could still be seen everywhere, such as here at this flower stall.

He wasn't sure how he felt about the transformation of his homeland. He would have preferred the EAC to be entirely eradicated and the Isles to return to exactly as they had been in his childhood. But no one could change the past. The BI of history was gone forever, as were all the historical versions of the Isles before it, right back to Arthur's time and beyond. The invaders couldn't be forced to leave or change their behavior without more conflict, bloodshed, and deaths. He supposed this way was the lesser of two evils.

He paid for the flowers, and the seller tucked the money into her belt.

"What are they?" he asked.

"Roses and carnations." She paused before continuing, "She'll say yes, sir. I can feel it in my bones. The Old Ones are smiling on you."

"Thank you. I hope so."

A short while later, he was walking up the road where

Taylan lived. The houses rose in ranks up the hillside, nearly identical and fronting directly onto the street in the old style. He stepped to her door, took a deep breath, and pressed the buzzer.

Then, in a quick afterthought, he darted to the side of the house and placed the flowers on the ground around the corner. So much time had passed since he'd seen Taylan and he'd told her not to wait for him. If she'd moved on, as she probably had, he didn't want to embarrass her.

He made it back to the door just as it opened.

A young girl stood there, about twelve or thirteen, her eyebrows lifting in surprise at his sudden appearance.

"Is Taylan Ellis here?"

The girl looked at him uncertainly. Not answering him, she turned and called inside, "There's a strange man at the door. A soldier."

Strange man?

He'd come straight here after disembarking from the *Dauntless*, not wasting time on changing out of uniform. He didn't correct her mistake about his service.

Another girl appeared in the doorway, or rather a young woman. She appeared to be twenty or so.

"I'd like to see Taylan," he explained. "Is she home?"

The woman looked him up and down before replying, "She's out the back in the garden. You can go around the outside." She pointed to the path.

As she closed the door the sound of giggling escaped.

He followed the path down the side of the house to the lawn at the end. The morning sun cast the path in shadow but shone brilliantly on the grass. He stood in the shade.

It was a long garden, and at the end two figures were sparring with staves. They were wearing protective helmets, but he recognized Taylan instantly. He knew the way she fought, her expertise lending unmistakable economy, power, speed, and grace to her movements. He remembered the time Colbourn and he had watched her fight Abacha in the *Valiant's* gym, and the brigadier had snatched a child's jewelry from her neck.

Who was she sparring with this time?

As he watched, his tenuous hope began to fade. Her partner was a man. He was good, though not as good as Taylan. She'd found a friend with shared interests. The question was, how close were they?

He watched the match, uncertain. Should he stay and wait until they were finished or should he leave now and avoid an encounter that could be awkward for all three of them? Maybe it would have been better to mail her to tell her he was back and then let her take the lead. He'd been impulsive and overly optimistic, which wasn't his style. He should have thought things through better.

There was a thud and an *Ow!*

Taylan had broken through her opponent's defense and landed a blow on the side of his head. The man staggered and dropped his staff. The ends of their weapons were padded, but the hit had clearly hurt.

Taylan also dropped her staff and leapt over to her partner. "I'm sorry! I'm so sorry. Does it hurt?" She held his head and peered into his eyes before hugging him.

Wright smiled sadly as hope departed. The man was clearly more to her than just a sparring partner. She would never have cared about Abacha or any other Marine getting hurt in a practice fight. It came with the territory.

He turned to leave.

"*Wright!*"

When he looked back she was racing down the long garden, ripping off her helmet and throwing it down. She reached him in a few seconds and bounded up like a puppy, wrapping her arms around his neck and her legs around his hips, nearly bowling him over.

He held onto her tightly in silence as seconds passed.

She was sweaty and her hair was a mess and he loved her.

"You're back," she said. "I can't believe it. Why didn't you tell me you were coming? How long has it been?"

"Nine years and five months." He could have told her how many weeks and days too, but it seemed excessive.

She let go of him and dropped to the ground. "Look at you!" She cupped his face in her hands. "You don't look any different. You haven't aged at all." She gasped and said softly "*Oh!*" before ducking her head. "But I have."

"It's okay. I had a few years on you, now you have a few on me. It's fine."

She looked up.

He kissed her forehead.

She touched the spot self-consciously. "I have a wrinkle there, right? You just kissed my wrinkle."

He bent to kiss her on the lips.

There was a small cough.

The man Taylan had been sparring had walked over and was standing nearby with his helmet under his arm, looking mildly embarrassed. Noticing Wright looking at him, he held out his hand. "I'm—"

"Patrin," Wright finished for him, shaking his hand. "It took me a moment. At the risk of sounding clichéd, my, you've grown."

"He has, hasn't he?" said Taylan, touching her son's shoulder. "And he hasn't stopped yet. It wouldn't surprise me if he ended up as big as Arthur. How is Arthur, by the way?"

"Not too bad. Wait, I have something for you."

He went to retrieve the flowers.

～

His clothes felt strange as he sat down to dinner with Taylan's family that evening. She'd persuaded him to print some civvies to wear so he would *look like a normal person*. The home printer was a bit of a luxury, she'd explained, bought courtesy of Lorcan Ua Talman's funds, on which they'd all been living in modest comfort since leaving the *Dauntless*.

They ate quietly. The excitement of the day seemed to have exhausted everyone. Except Wright wasn't exhausted so much as overwhelmed. It wasn't only the happiness and relief of seeing Taylan again and discovering she still felt the same toward him, it was something else.

As he ate, he realized it was the fact he was with a family, a happy, loving family he could be a part of, one day, with luck. Even when he'd gone to live with his best friend after his parents kicked him out, he'd never had this. He'd always known the arrangement was temporary.

Though his mouth was empty, he swallowed. He put down his knife and fork, unable to go on.

Taylan put her hand over his and smiled at him.

He swallowed again to try to make his voice sound normal. "It's delicious, but I can't eat any more."

"I'm glad you like it. The potatoes and peas are from the garden."

"Really? That's great. You're a fantastic cook."

"Thanks. I try my best."

A blob of mashed potato hit her in the face.

The young woman, who Wright had learned was called Carys, had thrown it.

A peal of laughter burst from Taylan as she wiped off the potato. "I didn't cook it. Carys did. She's the fantastic cook. I'm only pretty good."

"I'm not sure I'd say that," said Patrin.

"Hey, you better be careful what you say," Taylan retorted, "we're sparring again tomorrow, remember?"

Wright hadn't figured out exactly who Carys was. He hadn't recognized Kayla when he'd seen her at the door as she'd only been three or four at the meeting on the *Dauntless*, but now it was clear who she was. Carys was a little too old to be another of Taylan's children and she'd only ever mentioned having two.

As if reading his mind, Taylan said, "Carys helped me out a lot in the early days after we came back to the BI. I don't know what I would have done without her."

"You helped me too," Carys replied quietly. "You took me in."

"Of course I did," said Taylan. "What else would I do? If it wasn't for you…"

The pleasant atmosphere in the room dried up and expressions turned somber.

"Carys's mam and dad died in the war," said Kayla artlessly. "When she found out, she came to live with us."

Patrin frowned at his sister. "Carys saved our lives when we were with the Crusaders. Don't you remember?"

Kayla shook her head.

"Who's ready for dessert?" Carys asked brightly, standing up and beginning to gather the empty plates.

"Let me," said Wright.

"No, you're a guest," Carys protested.

"Sit down," Taylan told her. "Wright and I will do it together."

"Why do you call him that?" asked Kayla. "Wright's a surname, isn't it? I never heard anyone called Wright as a first name."

"Kayla, think before you speak," Patrin admonished. "That's the second time you've put your foot in your mouth."

"I was only asking!"

"Come on," Taylan said to Wright as her children began to bicker, "we can get some peace and quiet in the kitchen."

"Okay," he replied. "I need to speak to you privately about something anyway."

She gave him a worried look.

When they reached the kitchen carrying the stacked plates and dirty cutlery, she said, "This better not be about me having anything more to do with the Royal Marines. I was kinda hoping you were going to resign. How long have you served? Do they count the time as it passed while you were aboard ship or here on Earth?"

He put down his plates and took hers before depositing them on the work surface.

Then he kissed her.

Strains of the children's argument floated through from the dining room, interspersed with Carys's tired requests for them to shut up.

When the kiss was over, Taylan said, "Nice change of subject. Now, what was it you wanted to talk to me about?"

～

A SHORT WHILE LATER, they returned to the dining room. The children's squabble was over and Patrin was showing Kayla and Carys a bruise on his arm—rather proudly, it seemed.

"Wright wants to talk to you about something," Taylan announced.

She'd listened to his explanation carefully but, unusually, he had found it hard to gauge her reaction. Perhaps she was waiting to hear what the others said before giving her answer.

He pulled out a chair and sat down. Resting his elbows on the table and clasping his hands together, he began, "It's like this. Everything in the universe is connected..."

Taylan and Wright's story continues in...

THE DEFIANT

AUTHOR'S NOTES

Hello again faithful reader. Here we are at the end of book five of the Star Legend series. Only one more book to go. I hope you've enjoyed Taylan and Wright's story so far. I suppose as you're here, you have!

Special thanks to the shipmates who make the Star Legend series possible, especially Liza Wood, Mike Phillips, Mike Paddick, Alex Green, and the Review Crew.

If you're interested in hearing about some of the influences on and inspiration for *The Dauntless*, read on.

The Outback

If you've read my bio you'll know I describe myself as British-Australian. Though I was born in the UK I lived in Melbourne for many years and became an Australian citizen, hence my interest in and love for the Lucky Country. One story that fascinates me is the Burke and Wills expedition, which attempted to cross the continent south to north and back again. I'll leave you to find out how things turned out, but the tale served as inspiration for Taylan and Arthur's trek through the outback.

Kevin

We don't need to talk about Kevin very much. I wouldn't presume to speak on behalf of the Aboriginal people about them or their culture, but as the original Australians I felt they deserve a place in the story. One small point is Kevin's mention of his auntie. He almost certainly means an Elder rather than one of his parents' sisters, but Taylan wouldn't know that and he wouldn't bother to explain.

Arthur's Tattoos

Little is known about the tattooing practices of Arthur's period, but it's fun to speculate, right? What we do know through the writings of Roman historians, is that Britons loved to decorate their bodies. In fact, the name Britain derives from the Celtic word Pretani, which means painted ones. My guess is that we made the skin paintings permanent and the tattoos had decorative and spiritual purposes, the same as today.

Guinevere

Fun fact: the name Guinevere means white fairy or white phantom. An odd coincidence. It's the Norman French translation of the old Welsh Gwenhwyfar. The modern English version is Jennifer. I used to be very pleased about that when I was a kid and, to be honest, I still am.

If you'd like to read the final Star Legend book, *The Defiant*, a few weeks earlier than it will appear on Amazon, become a Patreon supporter at https://www.patreon.com/JJGreenAuthor

To chat about the series or meet other readers, come along to the Starship JJ Green Shipmates Facebook group. I'd love to see you there.

Sign up to my reader group for exclusive free books, discounts on new releases, review crew invitations and other interesting stuff:

https://jjgreenauthor.com/free-books/